NICK EAST

AGENT WEASEL

AND THE ...NG

HODDER

WINDTOP HILL

THE ROOKERY

BEAVER DAM

REED RUSH POND

GARRETT'S FARM

BIG OAK

BADGER WOOD

THE MEADOW

THE UNITED WOODLANDS

LOOK OUT FOR AGENT WEASEL'S OTHER ADVENTURES!

HODDER CHILDREN'S BOOKS

First published in Great Britain in 2021 by Hodder and Stoughton

1 3 5 7 9 10 8 6 4 2

ISBN 978 1 444 94532 4

Printed and bound in Great Britain by Clays Ltd, Elcograph S.p.A.
The paper and board used in this book are made from wood from
responsible sources

MIX
Paper from
responsible sources
FSC
www.fsc.org
FSC® C104740

Hodder Children's Books
An imprint of Hachette Children's Group
Part of Hodder and Stoughton
Carmelite House
50 Victoria Embankment
London EC4Y 0DZ
An Hachette UK Company
www.hachette.co.uk
www.hachettechildrens.co.uk

I HAVE SET THIS MAD WEASELLY CAPER IN MY FAVOURITE SEASON OF THE YEAR — SPRING! AND BY THE TIME THIS BOOK IS PUBLISHED, IT WILL ALMOST BE UPON US AGAIN. SOON, WE WILL CHEERFULLY RAMBLE THROUGH THE COUNTRYSIDE, DODGING SQUISHY COW PATS, WITH THE SIGNS OF NEW LIFE ALL AROUND. FOR ME, THIS SEASON MOSTLY BRINGS TO MIND HAPPY HOURS SPENT WITH FAMILY AND FRIENDS IN THE WARM SPRING SUNSHINE. SO I DEDICATE THIS BOOK TO THEM AND TO YOU AND TO THE JOYFUL TIMES AHEAD. N X

In a forgotten corner of the countryside
lies a small green wood, much like any other.
But take a closer look and it is far from ordinary.
For this is the United Woodlands – home of
Agent Weasel, legendary super-spy. A place full
of adventure, mystery – and an incredibly
wide variety of edible nuts.

CHAPTER 1

When spring sprang in the United Woodlands, it was usually with a *BOIIIIIING!* And this year was no different. After a long, chilly winter, things had turned in the blink of an eye. The air was piny fresh, the trees were flushed with green, and the birdies were chirping their feathery little heads off. Mother Nature was a wonderful thing indeed.

The celebrated super-spy Agent Weasel was lying on the lush banks of Babble Brook. Well, 'celebrated' might be stretching the truth a little – but certainly highly thought of. And if not highly thought of, definitely, er, well known!

He half dozed in the midday sun, a wide, satisfied smile on his chops. There was nothing like the gentle hum of a warm spring day.

TUG, TUG, TUG! The fishing line tied to Agent Weasel's toe twitched gently. He peeked through a half open eyelid. *Hmmm! Probably just snagged on some pondweed*, he thought.

Weasel hoped to catch a minnow or two for supper that evening, although he was not that

bothered. The tasty niff of sizzling slug burgers wafted over from Doorkins's barbecue spot below a shady yew tree.

Doorkins Dormouse was Weasel's best chum in the entire world. And this morning he sported a rather fine and lofty chef's hat. He busied himself happily flipping the burgers with a skilled flick of the wrist. It smelt DEEE-LICIOUS and Weasel breathed in the mouth-watering whiff.

Dreamily, he thought back to a couple of days ago. It was hard to imagine such

SIZZLE
SIZZLE

a different scene. Heavy rain had battered the United Woodlands into a right soggy old mess. The Beavers' dam at Reed Rush Pond was fit to burst. And burst it would have, if not for the quick thinking of WI6.

Weasel worked for WI6 – it stood for Woodland Intelligence. Nobody really knew what the six stood for, but it made the name sound cool and official, so they kept it in anyway.

Weasel had been ordered to squelch up north with a team of rather damp and bedraggled animals. Their mission: to help Mother and Father Beaver fix up the extremely leaky dam at Beaver Lodge.

The kindly beavers were dear friends and Weasel was determined to lend a paw in any way he could. But this had been a particularly tricky job.

They'd just about managed to stack enough branches and slap on enough claggy mud to hold back the water. But the slightest twitch of a gnat's eyebrow and the whole thing would have gone, swamping the United Woodlands in a massive mega flood! So everyone crossed their paws and hoped for the best.

And the next day – HEY PRESTO – the rain stopped and the sunshine pushed the clouds away!

TUG, TUG, TUG! The line around Weasel's toe pulled again. Then … *SCRUNCH!* A sheet of paper unexpectedly blew straight into the super-spy's face. He peeled it off and squinted in the bright sunshine.

THE ROBBER KING
RULES.
LONG LIVE
THE ROBBER KING.

What on earth is this twaddle all about?
he wondered. He didn't know the Woodlands
had a king, let alone a robber one.

'Medium or well done, Weasel?' It was
Doorkins; he tottered up, waving his barbecue
tongs like a wand. In fairness, they probably
were pretty magical – Doorkins's burgers were
the best Weasel had ever tasted.

'Tut-tut-tut, littering!' moaned Doorkins. 'I gathered a bunch of those to start my barbecue this morning.'

Weasel looked at the dormouse in surprise. Had someone been throwing these bits of paper all over the woods? Littering in the United Woodlands was a big NO-NO, and whoever had done it would be in for a stern telling-off.

'CHAT-CHAT!' came a strange cackling laugh from the tree across the bank.

Weasel noticed a wild beady black eye staring from between the leaves. 'HEY, is this anything to do with you?' he said, waving the bit of paper at their nosy neighbour.

No answer.

Doorkins shrugged. 'Your burger, Weasel, medium or well—?' But before Doorkins had finished his sentence – 'YEEEOOOW!' Weasel cried.

A powerful tug on the super-spy's toe had dragged him from the bank and – *SPUUUUURLOSH!* – straight into the briskly flowing Babble Brook.

SHIVERING STICKLEBACKS, talk about a shock. Even though spring had most definitely sprung, Babble Brook still had a wintery chill. Freezing-cold water shot up Weasel's nostrils as he was hauled along, submerged. Now if you've ever greedily bitten into an ice lolly, you'll know how painful this is. ICE-CREAM HEADACHE!

Suddenly Weasel's bottom bumped something hard and rock-like. Probably a rock, his super-spy brain thought, just as he bounced out of the water and into the air.

Briefly, he glimpsed Doorkins dashing along the bank. The dormouse shook his barbecue tools wildly above his head, shouting as he went. But before he could see at what or whom his best chum was squealing, Weasel was pulled back into the icy water and straight into a clump of bulrush reeds – OOOOOF! Keeping his legs crossed would have probably been the best plan.

It occurred to Weasel that this was certainly no diddy minnow hauling him along at a brisk rate of knots. It was far too powerful and speedy. For one dreaded moment he thought: *PIKE!* Which, if you don't know, is:

A VERY LARGE FISH,
WITH VERY BIG TEETH,
AND A VERY HUGE APPETITE.

Weasel had come face to face with these fearsome creatures before. And he was not keen to meet one again. YICKERTY-YIKES, the idea made him shudder.

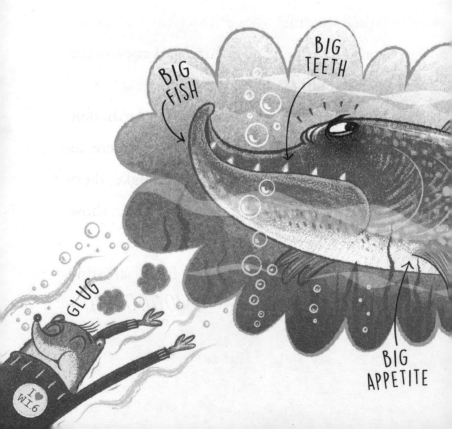

BIG FISH

BIG TEETH

BIG APPETITE

GLUG

I ♥ WI.6

Straining to lift his head for a peek, Weasel unexpectedly bounced up on a choppy little wave. To his surprise, he was now sitting completely upright, skimming along the water on his bottom. With a perfect view upstream, he could see a sleek furry body break the surface every so often. PHEW-WEE! Not a pike then, he decided in relief.

'STOOOOOP!' cried Doorkins suddenly. He pointed to four large lumps of rock in the stream ahead.

SUFFERING SEDGEWEED – the Babble Brook stepping stones! Unless you were as thin as a particularly skinny grass snake, there was no way you were squeezing between those big solid rocks.

In an instant the sleek furry creature sploshed to a halt, but – *SWOOOOOSH!* –

Weasel unfortunately did not.

He flew across the water's surface, straight at his mystery towing partner, and launched up its long back ... into the air. It was a jump any world champion water skier would have been proud of. *PING* went the fishing line as it snapped in two.

SWISH

Then …

KERRUNCH!

CHAPTER 2

Weasel came round with stars dancing in front of his eyes. Had that really just happened? One minute he was relaxing by the stream, soaking up the spring sunshine ... and the next he was ploughing through ice-cold water, with Doorkins's delicious slug burgers left far behind.

The hapless super-spy cleared his vision with a shake of the head.

Looking around, he found himself slumped over a fence rail high above Babble Brook. The fence, he knew, belonged to Farmer

Garrett, and marked the edge of the United Woodlands. As he glanced over to the right he saw Hedgequarters, the WI6 mission control. It happened to be based in a large hawthorn hedge, hence the name.

'CHITTER-CHITTER CHAT-CHAT-CHAT!' There it was again, that cackle. Weasel snapped his head round just in time to see a black shadow disappear up a close-by tree. He felt somebody was having a good old laugh at this tricky pickle he was in.

'WEEEEEEASEL, are you all right up there?' cried a voice from below.

Wearily he looked down again. Of course, it was Doorkins, standing on the bank next to a pair of webbed and furry paws. Weasel could not quite see who was attached to them. Stretching out for a better view, he suddenly began to lose his balance.

An unsettling flutter raced through Weasel's tummy. *PARP!* An unplanned bottom squeak sneaked out!

Oh, why always me? he thought, slipping headfirst towards the fast-flowing water below. But his back paw caught on the wooden fence rail and now the poor woodland super-spy was dangling upside down by his VERY sore big toe. The one still tightly wrapped in fishing line and which was turning a worrying shade of blue!

This was not going to end well, Weasel feared.

And with that, the toe popped off the fence and down he went. 'YAAAAAAAAAAR!' *THWUMP!*

Weasel wasn't expecting a soft velvety *THWUMP*, but more a huge soggy *SPLOSH!* But it appeared he had not belly-flopped into the freezing-cold Babble Brook after all. He seemed to be cuddled up against something warm and fuzzy. Instinct made him snuggle in like a baby kit. Weasel squeezed an eye open and stared into a wide, intelligent face, which teasingly fluttered its long eyelashes. Weasel smiled dozily – then suddenly came to his senses.

'AHEM! MAJOR O!' he exclaimed,

jumping from his rescuer's arms all of a fluster.

'Hello, me 'andsome, don't go getting all shy on me now, will you?' replied the tall sleek figure with a strong west-Woodlands accent.

Oh, what a PLONKER you are, Weasel scolded himself. The masterful swimming, the streamlined sleek body, the furry webbed paws. It could only be one creature! And that was Major Omega, or Major O for short.

She was an otter and a very elegant glossy one, at least four times the size of Weasel. She was powerful, as sharp as a thorn and a member of the elite Special Otter Squadron, or SOS to you and me.

She specialised in underwater missions, but was just as capable on dry land. A right old clever clogs, you might say. And she could be a little loud when the mood took her. But really

Major O was the salt of the earth and would do anything to help her fellow animal.

'I have to say, Agent Weasel, you were nearly splatted as flat as a very flat flat-fish then.' The otter smirked. 'What were you doing up there anyway?' She pointed to the fence rail high above their heads.

Weasel realised the Major had no idea she'd just dragged him quarter of a mile down Babble Brook, over its rocky bottom, through the bulrushes and up into the air like a weasel-shaped kite. And it was probably best if it stayed that way.

Doorkins had obviously come to the same conclusion and had climbed up the fence post behind the otter's back. He was twiddling around, secretly trying to unhook the fishing line from the Major's fur.

'Well, I have you to thank for my un-splatted appearance, Major,' Weasel replied with a nervous glance at Doorkins. 'It was just a … routine inspection. Got to keep our fences in tip-top condition, you know!'

The otter gave him a puzzled frown. 'Hmmm! Well, I'd love to stand here and chat, me old mucker. But I have an urgent report to make at Hedgequarters,' she said. 'It might be of interest to you too?'

Weasel's eyebrows rose with excitement.

'I can't say too much,' said Major O. But then of course she did. 'Shedloads of strange robberies have been happening all over the place in the last few days.'

'Strange, in what way?' asked Weasel.

'Well … the culprit has left absolutely no trace and all the pinched stuff has reportedly been, er … very shiny.'

'Like diamonds, gold … silver?' he said eagerly.

'More like toe-clippers, teaspoons and bottle openers,' replied the otter.

Weasel scratched his white furry chin. He looked down at the soggy bit of paper still gripped in his paw. Robber King, robberies … hmmm, could there be a link? Well, it looked like his day off was over.

'Sounds right up my street, Major,' replied Weasel, secretly waving to Doorkins to get down quickly. But somehow his friend was

now tangled in a mess of pondweed and fishing line. 'SHALL WE?' boomed Major O, marching off and dragging poor Doorkins along behind her as she went.

Oh, not again, thought Weasel. He took a deep breath and was about to scamper after his unfortunate fumbling friend when he suddenly felt he was being watched. Was it that black beady eye again?

Weasel looked up at Hedgequarters. And there on a high platform stood H – the head-honcho hedgehog at Woodland Intelligence. She must have seen everything. And she did not look best pleased.

OH, GOOSEGOGS PRESERVE US, he despaired. *I'm going to get a serious earful for this*. Weasel trudged off wearily, following the strange procession towards HQ.

CHAPTER 3

WI6 Hedgequarters stood on the junction between Babble Brook and Farmer Garrett's cow field. It was made up of thick, prickly hawthorn hedge, well trimmed and groomed all year round. Bits of wooden fence weaved in here and there, with the tallest post including a rather impressive circular landing pad. Birds of all kinds flew in and out throughout the day. But in times of emergency, it also doubled as a particularly fine lookout point over the surrounding countryside.

Animals could be seen scurrying about

through gaps in the hedge. But any day soon hawthorn blossom would burst forth, completely covering WI6 in a blanket of white flowers – which was always a sight for sore eyes after a long cold winter.

Weasel trudged up to the HQ main entrance behind the confidently strutting otter, who was still unknowingly dragging along Weasel's dormouse chum. Doorkins had quit his struggle and now lay back to enjoy the ride.

A large badger stood stiffly to attention guarding the way in. Badgers were particularly useful at this type of job. They were wide, sturdy and a little bit menacing.

The big gruff creature gave a quick nod to Major O as she passed straight through. He didn't notice Doorkins being hauled along behind the striding otter. Weasel went to

follow them, but was halted by a huge black paw across his chest.

'Do you 'ave any form of hi-dentification, SIR?' growled the badger guard with a frown.

'Er ... not on me – n-no,' answered Weasel, a little puzzled. He'd been going in and out of Hedgequarters every day for as long as he could remember – his face and top-notch reputation was usually enough to get him in. He arched his eyebrows and flashed his best spy-like smile.

'We've got a right one 'ere, Bill,' said the bulky badger into a radio intercom.

In an instant, an equally sizable badger barged out of the entrance, standing shoulder to shoulder with the first. They both snapped on a pair of rubber gloves and rather too keenly barked, 'BODY SEARCH!'

'GULP! Now look here, you chaps, I'm—!' But before Weasel could complete the sentence his arms and legs were forcibly spread out, and the badgers roughly patted him down with their big beefy paws. Flabbergasted, the WI6 super-spy was utterly lost for words.

''Ere, what's this then? Looks dangerous to me,' exclaimed one badger, pulling out a large rubber bathroom plunger from beneath Weasel's jumper.

'W-well, i-i-it's ...' stuttered Weasel, struggling to explain.

'AND THIS!' cried the other one, holding up a ripe pineapple, yanked from the same place. 'Hmmm, looks like a bomb, don't it!' he mumbled.

In moments a big pile of jumbled objects had appeared on the ground. The pullover was a special WI6 one, of course. When Agent Weasel got in a terrible fix, a quick rummage up there could produce a helpful gizmo or two. And he wished to HIGH HOLLYHOCKS he had the correct item now, if only to whack these two nincompoops over the head with!

'Hmmm! This is very worrying. Very worrying indeed,' agreed the badgers, as they looked over the pile of junk.

'What utter POPPYCOCK!' cried Weasel as he began to lose his cool.

As you may or may not know, a weasel losing their temper can be serious. It can trigger what is known as a Weasel War Dance. Usually this happens when a weasel is threatened or angry. It involves anything from wild bottom shaking to knocking your opponent flat with a single blow.

And Weasel could feel the War Dance coming on. But he had to keep control – making a scene outside Hedgequarters' front entrance was just not on.

A bunch of chittering chaffinches had quickly gathered. Typical. These birds were always ready to stick their nosy beaks in for a bit of extra gossip.

'LET ME THROUGH, LET ME THROUGH!' said a firm voice from behind them.

To Weasel's relief it was his good friend and fellow spy, Agent Mole. She was a jolly old sort and always ready to help an animal in need.

'Hello, Weasel old chap,' she beamed, all bright-eyed and bushy-tailed. Not that she had much of either – her eyesight was quite poor and her tail far from bushy. 'I do apologise – new security, you know. Some of which is not quite up to scratch.' Mole frowned crossly at the two bulky badgers, who now stared at the ground in shame. 'Bit of bother in the United Woodlands at the mo, I'm afraid, Weasel,' she said in a rather unsettled tone. 'We're about to have a Code Red/Adder Level meeting in the HQ operations room!'

CODE RED/ADDER LEVEL! That hadn't happened since the dippy tea biscuits ran out a few months ago. Weasel shuddered at the thought. And in the HQ operations room! Weasel had never been invited there before. So this was serious – very serious indeed.

Suddenly the chaffinches burst into a chirping frenzy and darted to the safety of a tree. 'CAW-CAW-CAW.'

Weasel and Mole looked up. It was
a large flock of big black birds that
had spooked the chaffinches. As they flew high
overhead, little bits of paper fluttered down to
the ground, twisting like autumn leaves. One
landed right on Weasel's nose. Snatching it up,
he read the message:

WIG ARE A LOAD OF PANTS!
LONG LIVE THE ROBBER KING!

'How very dare they?' growled Weasel.

Then ... 'CHITTER-CHITTER CHAT-CHAT-CHAT!' It was that same teasing cackle again! There was a shadowy movement on a branch above.

Immediately Weasel dropped on to all fours and his bottom began to shake wildly – it was the Weasel War Dance! The insult to WI6 was just too much to bear and Weasel saw red. He pawed the earth, then shot up the tree towards the intruder like a fizzing rocket!

Before he knew it, Weasel was balancing at the end of a long spindly twig. Two scaly black feet gripped the branch above him. Without thinking (which was fairly usual when in a Weasel War Dance), he leapt up and grabbed a foot.

'SQUAWK! SQUAWK! SQUAWK!' What a racket!

SQUAWK

The din brought
Weasel out of his trance.
Then he noticed a glint
of gold around the
skinny leg. Was it a ring?
The feet began to lift from
the branch in a panicked flap.
It was a ring! Weasel squinted at
it. It said 'Corvy' in curly etched
lettering on the side.

As he looked up, two beady
black eyes scowled down

BOING

at him and a long pointy beak opened wide. 'WHO'S A PRETTY BOY THEN? WHO'S A PRETTY BOY THEN!' it screeched wildly.

Ah! Always nice to get a compliment, Weasel thought. Then the sharp beak pecked fiercely at his paws. YIKES! Weasel released his grip instantly and fell like a lead balloon.

'Have a nice trip, Agent Weasel. CHAT-CHAT-CHAT!' cackled the squawky voice as it disappeared in a flash of black and white.

This tittering fiend knew his name! Could this be the Robber King?

THWUMP!

Weasel had landed on something soft and furry rather than hard ground. It was the two security badgers, now lying in a crumpled heap under the WI6 super-spy.

'Weasel!' cried Mole as she scampered up.

'Are you in one piece?'

'Well, it appears so — thanks to these two gentlemen breaking my fall.'

Mole helped Weasel up with a big spade-like paw. Mole was an underground digging expert, and her massive shovel paws were the fastest in the whole of the United Woodlands. Weasel had seen it for himself — she'd dug them out of some very tricky scrapes.

'Come on, let's get inside,' said Mole, glancing up at the sky. 'And you two nitwits get this lot cleared away!' She waved at the scattered bits of paper and the pile of stuff they had taken from Weasel's pullover.

The two flattened badgers groaned and nodded sheepishly.

As they walked towards Hedgequarters, Weasel nearly tripped over his large rubber bathroom plunger. He grabbed it, shoving it back up his WI6 spy pullover. Suddenly he thought, *EEW; did I use it to unblock the loo last week? Oh well, not to worry, surely it'll be useful for something.*

The pair walked through the entrance into HQ, Weasel pondering his tussle with the mysterious chattering fiend. Who was 'Corvy', and could this be a link to the Robber King?

CHAPTER 4

Inside WI6 Hedgequarters, there was some serious hustle and bustle going on. Animals scurried to and fro through the large open lobby area. Some scampered up the thick central hawthorn trunk, where smaller branches spread to the upper floors. Others went down the warren holes to the underground boffin labs and top-secret operation rooms.

WHIZZZZ! Weasel ducked as messenger-moths darted overhead, carrying reports on tiny rolls of paper.

He thought fondly of Muriel, his personally

trained elite homing moth. She was away visiting family at a chrysalis-hatching celebration. Weasel hoped she'd be back soon. He missed the sound of her fluttering wings … and the munched holes in his best wool-wear.

Talking about missing friends, Doorkins waddled up, still in a bit of a taffle.

'Did you catch anything, dear chap?' chortled Mole, pointing at the fishing line tangled around his body.

'Ah, hello, Mole. Just, er, a big confident otter.' Doorkins pointed to Major O, who stood deep in conversation with a couple of tree sparrows. Weasel instantly recognised them as Special Branch – named in honour of the particularly special hazel tree in which they lived. These little birds were brilliant aerial spies. They could spot an ant on a puffball from a hundred metres.

RECEPTION

Was their conversation something to do with the recent robberies? It was difficult to tell; reading beaks at this distance was a tricky business.

'Let's not keep H waiting,' Mole reminded him. 'You know what a fuss-pants she can be.'

Weasel knew only too well. H, the head honcho

PING

at W16, liked everything done completely by the book. Which meant the W16 SPY MANUAL, a large encyclopaedia on how to spy. Weasel much preferred a good old swashbuckling adventure story. His style of spying was more off-the-cuff and this did not always go down too well with the WI6 leader.

Warren Entrance 101 led directly to the WI6 operations room deep below ground. Major O scurried along urgently on all fours. The flickering light bulbs above swung to and fro as she passed. Weasel, Mole and Doorkins struggled to keep up.

They were quite relieved when their speedy

hike came to a halt. The group stood in front of a large round door. It had been cut from a section of oak tree, year rings spiralling from its centre and thick bark crusting the outer edge.

Weasel noticed a small box mounted on the tunnel wall to the right. It said 'LEAF PASS' in bold official-looking letters.

Mole fished around in her pocket. 'Hmmm, was it an ash or beech leaf today? Er, beech, I think.' She pulled out a green tear-shaped leaf and stuck it into a wide slot on top of the box. 'More pesky security,' muttered Mole, shrugging her shoulders.

MUNCH–MUNCH–MUNCH came from inside. After a few moments, a rather plump caterpillar stuck its head out of the top. As it chewed away thoughtfully, the caterpillar gave a curt nod and the hefty door rolled open.

'Phew! It was beech after all.' Mole beamed.
'Leaf security changes daily – you have to keep
on your toes.'

Ingenious, thought Weasel. *What will
those Boffin Bunnies come up with next?*

The Boffin Bunnies were a bunch of very
smart rabbits. It was their brains behind most,
if not all, of the WI6 gadgets and thing-a-

me-whatsits. Spy life would be so much more difficult without them.

They walked through the door into a small and cramped room. Now Agent Weasel saw the WI6 operations room, he was not impressed at all. It felt more like a broom cupboard than a top-secret underground meeting place.

BANG! CRASH! CLANK!

'S-so s-sorry, everyone!' stuttered poor Doorkins. He'd tripped over on a bucket and mop by the doorway. Weasel helped his little chum back to his paws.

They all squashed into the damp musty space.

'OOF!'

'OUCH!'

'YEOW!'

Suddenly the heavy door rolled shut and it went dark.

'Brilliant!' groaned Weasel.

THUNK! CLUNK! There was an uneasy shift in the floor and a glare of bright light appeared from behind. A bit of a kerfuffle followed, as the group shuffled round to face the right way.

'EEK!'

'OOF!'

'Not my tail!'

'Well, this is more like it!' exclaimed Weasel.

Before them lay a rather impressive long but narrow room. It was pretty dark apart from a square of light projected on the wall at the far end, near a high-backed chair standing in the shadows.

'AH! Here you are AT LAST,' came an impatient grumble.

GULP! Weasel knew that voice and it sounded miffed. Extremely miffed.

CHAPTER 5

As their eyes adjusted to the light they saw a fine slate-topped table stretching the whole length of the room. Toadstool seats ran down either side.

Weasel's mouth began to water as he saw

a large teapot and a magnificent array of delicious-looking biscuits; he'd had nothing to eat since breakfast, and he'd missed out on Doorkins's yummy slug burgers.

But then he noticed the selection of small plaques lining the neatly dug walls. Each one displayed an odd little quote:

A DRY COWPAT IS A SAFE COWPAT

CLEAN PAWS FOR A CLEAR MIND

THE BEST BISCUIT IS A DUNKED BISCUIT

Well, Weasel certainly agreed with the last one, but he found the rest rather irritating.

'Admiring my little nuggets of wisdom, I see, Agent Weasel?' said the head-honcho hedgehog from the far end of the room.

'Ah, yes, H, er, very informative,' he replied hesitantly.

H raised an eyebrow and fixed him with a piercing stare. 'Right then, let's get down to business.'

Everybody pulled up a toadstool. Weasel sat opposite the ample tray of biscuits. He reached out a paw for one of his favourites – the stripy ones with icing on top, of course – when ... *WHAM!*

The WI6 boss slammed down a top-secret file on to the table. The animals jolted in shock. Dust drifted up through the light beam as H slowly opened the file.

Weasel gazed longingly at the tray of tasty nibbles.

'We are, how should I say it, in a bit of a pickle,' said the WI6 head honcho as she pulled out a piece of paper and held it up. It read:

THE ROBBER KING RULES!
LONG LIVE THE ROBBER KING!

Mole glanced at Weasel with her eyebrows raised. It was a good job H hadn't seen the most recent message about WI6 being a load of PANTS! She would go absolutely bonkers.

'THESE pesky leaflets have been dropped

all over our beautiful Woodlands,' said H through gritted teeth. 'And not only this thoughtless littering – there has been some thoughtless robbing as well!'

The hedgehog leader nodded to Major O.

The otter put a paw to her mouth and gave a quick shrill whistle. A projected map of the United Woodlands appeared on the wall behind the high-backed chair.

'Well, I'll get straight to the point, me old muckers – shiny stuff is going missing.'

Weasel noticed a little frown appear across Doorkins's brow.

'What kind of shiny stuff?' questioned Doorkins, pulling out his notebook and pencil from the small leather bag on his shoulder. Doorkins wrote a column for local newspaper the DAILY CONKER.

'No reporting, dormouse – this is strictly off the record!' barked the Major.

'Er, I think you'll find the mouse's name is Doorkins,' snapped Agent Mole.

'HUMPH!' puffed the large otter in annoyance.

Oh dear! Weasel wondered if Agent Mole and Major O were ever going to get on. 'So exactly what kind of, er, shiny stuff, Major O?' he chimed in quickly.

'The list is long, Agent Weasel. There have been break-ins all over the place!' The otter produced a long willow pointer and thrust it at the map. 'A treasured teaspoon collection here in Nettle Patch Corner, an antique flea comb in Dingy Dell, platinum nut-crackers at Oak Tree Rise. A pair of chrome claw-clippers from Little Thicket … the list goes on!'

'Ahem, and worst of all,' cut in Mole, 'reports confirm the priceless Starling Silver Nuts have been snatched from Principal Pine Marten's house!'

The Starling Silver Nuts were PPM's special symbol of office, worn round the neck of the acting Woodlands leader – mainly for posh occasions only, of course.

Grim news indeed, thought Weasel. Then the biscuits distracted him again; warily, he reached out for the tray but … *WHAM!* H thumped her fist down on the table. Weasel jumped from his toadstool with a start.

'I want every mammal, bird and insect out there on this one. If this is all down to the so-called Robber King, he must be caught and caught fast!' she snapped.

'It'll take some right proper detective work to crack this case, H,' declared the Major. 'This culprit is a tricky one and no mistake.'

Weasel thought about mentioning his cackling foe from that morning. But he was still way too taken with the glorious display of biscuits.

Looking over the top of her glasses with a firm stare, H pressed a button on a table-top intercom and barked, 'Boffin Bunny Kew to Operations Room 101 immediately!'

Weasel just nicely had his paw on a favourite stripy biscuit when … *CLUNK!* A section of the table began to rise, taking the tray of sweet delights with it.

'SUFFERING SHORTBREAD!' he mumbled.

Up through a hole where the biscuits had been appeared a thin grey rabbit. He had one bent ear and a large conker under his arm. It was Kew, an especially brainy Boffin Bunny. And, as with most Boffin Bunnies, he didn't say much – they were doers, not talkers. And the stuff they did was pretty blinking brilliant, it had to be said.

ZUMMMMMMMMM

SIGH

Kew nodded politely and set the sizable conker down on the table surface. He gently pushed on the conker's crown and the top section rose with a satisfying *SHWUMF.*

'A WI6 ADVANCED DETECTIVE KIT!' exclaimed Weasel.

He'd always wanted to get his paws on one of these. Neatly packed into its bottom half were jars, brushes, camera equipment and many other detecting treasures. And then he saw it – a magnificent shiny chrome magnifying glass ... WOW!

'Now you have the proper equipment, get me some proper results!' ordered the WI6 leader.

'Right, let's be off then!' said Weasel, snatching the detective kit from the table and making straight for the exit.

'Weasel – a word if I may?' called H.

Ah! He'd known this was coming. If only he'd moved a little faster. Passing the detecting kit over to Major O, he shuffled reluctantly back to the WI6 leader.

'So, Agent Weasel,' H said, studying him through squinty eyes. Weasel knew it was serious when she used his full title. 'I've been considering this for a few days.'

Uh-oh, here it comes, he thought – *a good old telling-off.*

'In light of this little scrape we find ourselves in, I think it's time you had full security clearance for WI6 HQ.'

'P-p-pardon?' spluttered Weasel in disbelief.

'Here's your ID passport with all the daily leaf codes.' She handed over a smart little booklet with the WI6 logo stamped on the front in gold lettering.

'Th-thank-you, ma'am.' He gave a short sniff and wiped his eyes, before turning to his colleagues.

'Oh and Weasel, before you go. No more blunders like that Babble Brook carry-on this morning, eh?'

Well, she had to go and spoil it all, didn't she? He marched off in a huff.

CHAPTER 6

Back in Hedgequarters lobby, the animals put their noggins together for a quick plan of action. They needed to find this Robber King – and fast!

Major O gave out the orders.

'All right, me dears, listen up,' she barked bossily. The animals pricked up their ears, apart from Mole, who just crossed her paws.

'Weasel, Doorkins – you bumble over to Principal Pine Marten's house, see if there's any sniff of those Starling Silver Nuts. I'll paddle upstream and check out the other robberies. And when we've got all the evidence we can – back here in time for tea. You could rustle us something up, eh, Mole?' The otter smirked.

Weasel cringed, half-expecting hot steam to shoot out of Mole's ears. Were these two ever going to get on?

Mind you, all this talk of tea was making his tummy rumble. Weasel quite fancied the pinecone crumble and ice cream on today's HQ canteen menu.

'Hey, why not catch a wood pigeon from the upper deck?' suggested Mole. 'It'll be much quicker than by paw.'

The outdoorsy bit on top of Hedgequarters was the best place to catch a passenger bird to any part of United Woodlands.

'What an absolutely top idea, Mole,' replied

Weasel enthusiastically.

Doorkins did not look quite so keen; flying was not really his thing. In fact, it made him feel decidedly queasy.

'Come on, old chum, let's go!' Weasel urged. With a quick cheerio to Mole, the pair dashed off up the central hawthorn trunk. Weasel held on tightly to the WI6 detective kit – there was no way this conker was leaving his paws. Both being expert climbers, it took them no time to reach the breezy upper deck.

'Ahhh! Look at that, Doorkins my friend,' breathed Weasel, taking in the magnificent countryside view. A crop of bright yellow rapeseed was just coming into flower in the field below. Hang on … hadn't a scarecrow been in that field for years? Where had it gone? Hopefully not another thing nabbed by the dastardly Robber King!

'Er, Weasel?' Doorkins pointed to a sign at the edge of the HQ landing pad, streaked with white bird poop.

WARNING!
FOR YOUR OWN SAFETY,
PLEASE STAY BEHIND THE WHITE LINE

Weasel looked down. He was standing on what appeared to be the wrong side of a thick white safety line.

Then suddenly ... *SPLATCH!!*
A big white glob of poop
splattered down the length
of his WI6
spy jumper.

'SQUELCHY BOGWARTS!' he cried in dismay.

'COOO-COOO!' came a call from above. A large heavy bird *THUNKED* down in the middle of the landing pad.

'Ah! Sorry about that, fella-me-lad,' boomed the pigeon. 'I gets a bit nervous landin' up 'ere on this tiny little thing. It's good luck, though – the bird poop, that is.'

If getting pooped on was good luck, then Weasel was not having much of it with his jumpers. The dry-cleaning bill was horrendous – but that was spy life for you. Well, it was if you were Weasel – Agent Weasel.

'Where can I take you two gents?' asked the tubby wood pigeon, adjusting his goggles and flight scarf ready for take-off.

Doorkins handed his super-spy friend a

mouse-sized handkerchief.

'Er … Little Thicket, with haste, my good bird,' replied Weasel, hopelessly dabbing at the gooey mess on his jumper.

'No bother – up you get, all part of the service.'

What, getting pooped on? thought Weasel. *Surely not?*

As the pair settled on to the pigeon's broad back, the bird glanced over his shoulder. 'Paws and tails in, ears down and safety belts on.'

'Er, what safety belts?' enquired Doorkins nervously.

The large bird ignored this. 'I'd like to welcome you to this Go-Pigeon flight P-4-2 – bound for Little Thicket. We will soon launch from this 'ere platform in a death-defying dive and cruise to a height of approximately—'

'What was that about a death-defying—

WAAAAAAAAAHH!' screeched Doorkins as they plunged from the upper deck, straight at the ground.

YEEEEHAAAAAAAA

Just as they were about to smack into the woodland floor, the pigeon swooped up into the tree canopy. 'YEEE-HAAA!' cried Weasel. 'WHAT A THRILL, EH, DOORKINS?' The poor little dormouse covered his eyes as he gripped on for dear life.

FLAP—FLAP—SHUMF!

'We 'ope you enjoyed your flight with Go-Pigeon. Please mind the gap as you leave the bird.'

They had landed in the tree directly above Principal Pine Marten's house, smack-bang in the centre of Little Thicket village, capital of the United Woodlands.

There was a bit of a commotion down below. A group of rowdy animals jostled about holding angry signs and shaking fists, furious about the robberies. PPM stood on the raised steps at the front door, waving in an attempt to calm the hullabaloo. It wasn't working.

As the two friends jumped down from the wood pigeon, Weasel asked, 'Before you go, old chap, ever heard of the Robber King?'

The hefty bird gulped with fear. 'Don't mention that name round here,' he said, quaking. 'They have beady eyes everywhere!'

'They?' questioned Weasel.

'I can't say no more – I might end up with me tail feathers plucked. Look to the Rookery,' he whispered and flapped off in, er, a bit of a flap.

The pair exchanged puzzled glances.

'Well, that went down like a trump in a bird-hide. Come on, Doorkins, let's get down there quick-smart!' Tucking the WI6 detective kit up the front of his jumper, Weasel scampered down the tree trunk, with Doorkins following close behind.

'Ah! Thank you for coming, Agent Weasel and er, Doorkins, isn't it?' PPM welcomed them as they jumped down on to the front steps of her grand residence. Pine martens have an important haughty sort of look about them – an ideal quality for a respected leader. Not that she was getting much respect at the moment.

'DUCK!' cried Weasel as a rotten gooseberry flew mere inches over their heads. *SPLATCH!* It hit the door just behind them. Then another … *SPLATCH!*

'As you can see, things are getting a bit sticky round here.' She pointed to the joggling signs in the boisterous crowd.

WHERE'S MY GRANNY'S SHINY STUFF? said one.

RABBITS AGAINST ROBBERY said the next.

I WANT MY TEA claimed another.

'Don't worry, PPM – we're on it,' vowed Weasel. 'We'll find out who's behind this and get the Starling Silver Nuts back!'

'See that you do, Weasel, I'm relying on WI6,' said PPM, standing grandly to her full height. 'I … must stay and face my public. I … must be a strong leader in this time of need, I—' *SPLATCH!* Her speech was cut short when a big squidgy blackberry hit her full in the face.

'Right, er … we'll get on and investigate, shall we?' Weasel winced. He and Doorkins crept into the house.

SQUISHY BLACKBERRY

WHERE'S MY GRANNY'S SHINY STUFF

HEY!

I WANT MY TEA

RABBITS AGAINST ROBBERY

I ♥ WI.6

PM

PPM's house was the biggest in the whole of the United Woodlands. As they entered, the pair were so distracted by its awesomeness they ran straight into the ribbons of sticky WI6 incident tape ... *SCRUNCH—CRACKLE—THWUMP!* They fell on to the floor, tangled in the stuff.

'AH-OO-OO-OH-ERM!' The more they struggled, the worse things got.

'Hang on, old chap.' Weasel scrambled to his feet. Doorkins was now taped to his back, facing in the opposite direction. A bit like a mouse-shaped rucksack.

'My second taffle today,' sighed poor Doorkins, remembering the fishing line earlier. Weasel staggered further into the room.

The noisy crowd could still be heard through the thick walls. Weasel hoped the Woodlands leader was coping!

The inside of the house was high and spacious. It was built around a huge upright walnut tree. Weasel spotted a hefty iron safe set into the tree's trunk. The door hung wide open and there was no sign of the Starling Silver Nuts — well, of course not, they had been pinched, hadn't they!

'Heeelloo — anybody there-there-there ...' echoed Weasel's voice eerily. Then ...

'LOOK OUT!' yelled Doorkins.

BOSH!

A swift black and white blur suddenly thumped into the duo and sent them sprawling across the fancy parquet floor. Everything became a bit fuzzy after that.

CHAPTER 7

Stars pinged and floated before poor Weasel's eyes. Yet again he shook his head, shooing away the tiny specks of light. This habit of bashing his noggin would have to stop. How much more could he take?

Then he realised he was staring up into a BIG BLACK BEADY EYE.

'WHO'S A PRETTY BOY THEN? WHO'S A PRETTY BOY THEN?' croaked the wild, raspy voice. 'Watch out, watch out, there's mischief about. WHO'S A PRETTY BOY THEN?'

With a sudden flap the beady eye was gone. Weasel looked up to see a dark shape darting through a high window. 'CHITTER-CHITTER CHAT-CHAT-CHAT!' went the same cackling call.

'ROLLICKING ROYAL RUFFIANS, he got away again, Doorkins!' growled Weasel ... but there was no reply! What had happened to his poor chum? He had been there a minute ago.

'UUUUMMM-UUUUMMM!'

What on earth was that strange muffled sound? It reminded Weasel of – AAARRGH, DOORKINS!

The unfortunate little dormouse was still strapped to the super-spy's back; he lay squashed under his weight.

Weasel instantly leapt up. Doorkins drew a deep breath ... *GASP*.

'Please accept my apology, old chap!' begged Weasel. 'Don't fret, I'll get us out of this ridiculous muddle.'

Struggling to his paws, Weasel hopped over to PPM's enormous oak desk. Amongst all the bits of paper and other official-looking odds and ends, there was a glint of something shiny. He grabbed the object with some difficulty – his arms still taped to his sides – and cried with delight, 'BINGO! A

letter-opener.' It looked to be made of silver, with a finely shaped duck's head handle. *Very nice*, he thought, *our burglar missed this one. I wonder if that thieving critter came back for it?*

Weasel began to hack at the tape immediately. 'Won't take a minute ... hold on, good buddy.'

'Er, Weasel, hang on, I'm going to ... drop ... OUCH!' squeaked the dormouse as he thumped to the ground.

'Oi, what's this?' Doorkins picked up something from the floor as he dragged himself up.

Weasel's eyes widened. 'Ah-ha! It looks like the gold ring I saw before.'

Doorkins looked a little puzzled.

'Can I, er, have a peek?' Weasel asked politely. Doorkins handed it straight over. It

 was definitely the same ring he'd seen earlier – it had the word 'Corvy' etched on the side.

'This is a very important clue,' claimed Weasel, going all showy and detective-like. 'In fact, this could belong to … THE ROBBER KING HIMSELF!'

'You mean that was …?' Doorkins pointed up to the high window.

'Yes, Doorkins, the one and only Robber King. Probably.'

Weasel felt it was time to get detecting. He put the ring carefully up his jumper, then rummaged around for the WI6 detective kit … EEK!

It was gone! If he'd lost it, H would have his paws for backscratchers!

'There, Weasel, there.' Doorkins pointed towards the tree trunk at the centre of the room. The detective kit had rolled over to the empty safe.

'THANK THE KNOBBLY NUTS … it must have popped out when that rotter knocked us flat,' Weasel blurted in relief.

As he picked it up, he noticed the conker was partly open. Everything seemed to be there. Apart from – NOOOOOOOOOOO – the beautiful shiny magnifying glass! Had that villain nicked it?

The two friends scurried round, looking for the precious item. It was nowhere to be found.

'GRRRRRRRRRR!' snarled Weasel. 'Wait until I get my paws on that stinker.'

If there were any more clues, they needed to find them and quick-smart. It would soon be teatime back at Hedgequarters, and Weasel did not want to miss the pinecone crumble and ice cream – not on your Aunt Nelly.

The pair got straight down to work. Doorkins would dust for paw prints and Weasel, without the … *SOB* … splendid magnifying glass, would search for small stuff with the WI6 detective tweezers.

They didn't get very far before …

'NAAAAAAAAR! It's no good, Weasel, this dang thing won't come off!' Doorkins was struggling with the lid of a big jar. On the label it said 'Doctor Pops's Most Excellent White Fingerprint Dust'.

'Ahem! Why don't YOU tweezer, my good mouse, and I'll carry on the dusting duties?' Weasel had gone all pompous – he was in full detective mode now.

A few moments later …

'NAAAAAR! TALK ABOUT JAMMED!' cursed Weasel. He gritted his teeth and tried with all his might. *POOOOOOOOOF!* The lid flew off and white powder went everywhere. Poor Weasel was covered from head to paw! He stood there and blinked in astonishment.

Then the door creaked open.

To Weasel's horror, a glistening purple lumpy paw gripped its edge. As the door swung fully open, it revealed the most horrible sight he had ever seen. Thick purple gloopy skin covered the thing's body. Slime trailed behind as it pushed the door shut. And the eyes were wide, wild and bloodshot!

Weasel could not help but scream, 'AAAAARGGGH!'

The purple gloopy creature screamed back, 'AAAAARGGGH!'

Doorkins popped up from behind the desk to see what all the fuss was about. 'Oh hi, PPM! I see the fruit-chucking got a little out of paw then,' he observed calmly.

'PRINCIPAL PINE MARTEN!' gawped Weasel in utter shock. 'I thought you were a dribbling bog-monster.'

YIKES!

UUUNHHHHHHH

'AGENT WEASEL! I thought you were a spooky ghost,' replied PPM, equally dumbfounded.

'Er, what is that noise?' asked Doorkins. He pricked up his super-dormouse ears. Doorkins could hear an acorn drop from the other side of the forest.

Weasel listened carefully – no … nothing. Then … ah, yes, was that a faint rumble? Then a bigger rumble and then, rather worryingly, an almighty rumble.

'It sounds like, it sounds like—?' PPM shook with the jitters.

'IT SOUNDS LIKE WATER!' cried Weasel. 'AND LOTS OF IT!'

The lower windows suddenly burst inwards and loads of bubbling, frothy water gushed into the room.

SWOOOOOOSH!

'FLOOOOOOD!'

howled Weasel.

CHAPTER 8

The water flowed to knee-height in seconds. Principal Pine Marten, who stood near the front door, panicked and went for the handle.

'NOOOOO!' cried Weasel at the top of his voice. But the warning came too late. *SWOOOSH*, the door flew open and tonnes more gurgling white water rushed in.

PPM went flying!

Pushed back by the galloping flood, she ploughed straight into poor Doorkins. *OOOOOF!* The two flailing animals shot into the open safe and the door *THUNKED* shut.

'AAAAAAAAARGH!' screeched Weasel.

The water level was rising quickly! He doggy-paddled furiously towards the disappearing safe, took a deep gulp of air and plunged underwater. It was strangely calm and still compared to the surface – apart from the odd bit of furniture bobbing past. With a swift kick of his paws, Weasel reached the submerged safe in an instant.

The huge iron door had a big numbered dial in the centre. Probably for putting in a secret code or combination – but Weasel didn't have the combination. Principal Pine Marten had it, but she was trapped inside with his best chum.

The spy felt a little twinge of panic. Urgently, he waggled the door handle next to the dial – it wouldn't budge.

BOM–BOM–BOM ... was that a knock? He put an ear to the door.

BOM–BOM–BOM ... there it was again.

HA! THANK THE LUCKY STARS, they were OK. But that air would run out quickly – it was a big safe but not that big.

Talking about air running out, Weasel's lungs felt fit to burst. The super-spy speedily kicked back to the surface.

'AAAAAAAH!' He breathed in deeply, taking in gobfuls of fresh air while looking round the room.

The roaring sound was gone and the water had stopped rising. Hmmm – a flash flood then, Weasel figured. YICKERTY YIKES! He immediately thought of the dam at Beaver Lodge – had it burst? If so, he hoped his good friends Mother and Father Beaver were OK.

Then he noticed PPM's desk floating nearby.

'Hmmm – what about this safe combination then?' he asked himself out loud. It could be in the desk, maybe? Popping underwater again, he tried all the drawers. Every one was LOCKED!

Then he noticed a strange tapping sound. *BIP–BOM–BOM–BOM–BOM, BIP–BIP–BOM– BOM–BOM, BIP–BIP–BIP–BOM–BOM, BIP– BIP–BIP* … it went on! There was something familiar about it. Weasel put his head back above water – it stopped. Then under again … *BIP–BIP–BIP–BOM–BOM.*

'AH-HA! That's Morse code – it must be Doorkins,' he gurgled excitedly, forgetting that he was still underwater. He came to the surface spluttering.

Morse code is an alphabet of dots and dashes Weasel had learnt at spy school. And of course good old Doorkins, being the excellent creature he was, knew it like the back of his paw.

Weasel took another deep breath and dived back down again. The tapping appeared to have stopped. He knocked briskly on the thick safe door and suddenly it was off again.

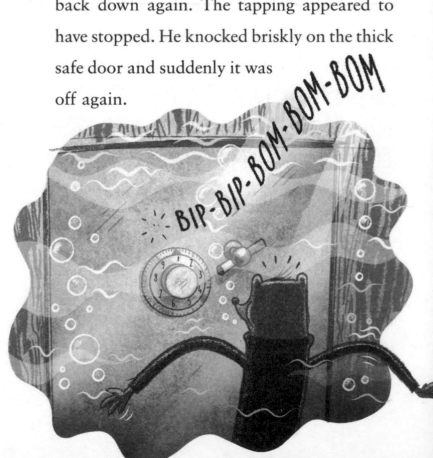

BIP-BIP-BOM-BOM-BOM

BIP–BOM–BOM–BOM–BOM – that meant number one.

BIP–BIP–BOM–BOM–BOM – number two.

BIP–BIP–BIP–BOM–BOM – number three.

BIP–BIP–BIP–BIP–BOM – number four.

One, two, three, four … was that the lock combination? If so, it was pretty rubbish – no wonder the Starling Silver Nuts were missing. He would have to have a word with PPM about sloppy code numbers.

CLICK–CLICK–CLICK–CLICK. Weasel turned the dial and pulled the handle. The door shifted a tiny way. He tugged with all his strength but it would not budge.

BOM–BOM–BOM! The knocking from inside became more frantic. *EEK!* Had water started gushing in?

Weasel tried to stay calm. He needed

something to pry open that door, and quick. Popping back to the surface, he feverishly looked for anything remotely useful ... the angle-poise desk lamp ... no ... a feather duster bobbed by ... NO, definitely not.

BAH! This was as unreliable as rummaging up his WI6 spy jumper! AH-HA! HIS WI6 JUMPER! That was it – the security badgers may have confiscated just about everything else, but he did have one item left.

TA-DAH! Weasel pulled out the large rubber bathroom plunger.

As he swam back down through the murky water, the knocking could still be heard. *BOM–BOM–BOM!* A good sign – or so he hoped!

Weasel thrust the plunger at the iron door. *THUNK!* It gripped instantly and he began to heave away.

After what seemed like ages, but was probably only a minute, the door hadn't budged! Poor Weasel's lungs screamed for air and he was running out of strength. But he couldn't give up now – Doorkins and PPM were relying on him.

Things began to go a bit wibbly-wobbly, his head started to spin and his vision went blurry.

Suddenly, something big and firm brushed against him. Two large webbed paws reached out and grabbed the plunger. And then, well, yes – everything went black ... AGAIN!

CHAPTER 9

Agent Weasel was relaxing on the banks of Babble Brook. The sunshine warmed his back and he chomped away on a big delicious slug burger – one of chef Doorkins's absolute best!

'Ah, what a day,' he sighed.

Then, without warning, a huge fish leapt from the water. It snatched the tasty snack right out of Weasel's paws with an enormous *GULP!*

'HEY!' he cried as it *SPLOSHED* back into the stream, soaking him from fur to skin.

'WEEEASEL! WEEEASEL!' called a familiar

voice from far away. As he turned to see who was calling him, the whole scene dissolved into woozy darkness – just like a dream.

BOSH, BOSH, BOSH. The next thing he knew, someone was bouncing up and down on his chest like a mad thing. Each thump caused water to spurt from his snout. He felt a bit like a weasel-shaped garden fountain. He sat up with a jolt and began to cough and splutter.

'WEASEL,
YOU'RE ALIVE!'
yelled Doorkins in relief as he hugged his life-
long best buddy.

'Y-yes, my friend, I think so,' he croaked.
'Th-thanks for the, er, what do you actually
call that?'

'CPR – cardiopulmonary resuscitation!'
replied the dormouse with a firm nod.

Hmmm! Unusual technique, Weasel
thought, *more suited to trampolining.* But

he was beyond pleased to see his little mousey pal in one piece.

'I must thank you for your brave efforts, Agent,' said Principal Pine Marten. Her jacket was still covered in squishy blackberry stains, although she did look slightly less terrifying now all the gunge had washed off.

They were floating on the desk in the middle of the flooded room.

Weasel smiled. 'Don't thank me, ma'am, I only— ' But before he could finish, there was a huge *SPLASH* and Major O's massive head burst from the water.

'AH! Good to see you back in the land of the living, me old mucker,' she boomed.

'Thank you, Major, I—'

'Ah! Always ready to help an animal in need, Weasel.' She modestly waved away his gratitude. 'Better stick THIS back up your jumper – might come in useful again.' She shoved the bathroom plunger into his paws and gave him a quick wink.

Weasel did as he was told. The otter was kind of pushy – but a very good sort at heart. 'I'm glad you showed up when you did.' He grinned. 'But I thought you were off checking out the other burglaries?'

'Well, that's a story an' a 'alf, me 'andsome,' she replied.

Major used her sweet-talk on everybody, Weasel knew that, but it always made him blush and go a bit hot under the collar. 'Ahem! I-I'd be interested to h-hear,' he stuttered.

The special-forces otter told them how she had gone north to investigate the other dastardly wrongdoings. There, she'd faced a number of overwrought animals who JUST WANTED THEIR PRECIOUS SHINY STUFF BACK!

PPM nodded in exhausted sympathy – she knew that feeling well. But for her it had included a good splattering of rotten fruit.

Major's journey had continued upstream to Reed Rush Pond, when it unfortunately came to an abrupt and catastrophic end in a HEAD-ON PRANG!

'GOSH! With what?' Doorkins gawped, wide-eyed.

'Well, it was the old beavers from Beaver Lodge, me bootie,' she replied.

Mother and Father Beaver had apparently left the lodge in a bit of a kerfuffle after their dam had been pummelled by a big bunch of thug-like birds.

Weasel thought back to the flock of litterbugs this morning – could it have been them?

'That's when we heard the rumble!' The otter shuddered. 'You should have seen it, Weasel – it was a wave the size of a hedge!'

Weasel had feared a burst dam all along. *It wouldn't have taken much to set that rickety old pile of sticks off*, he thought.

'That was the last I saw of the Beavers,' said the Major sadly.

Weasel was concerned for his friends – but beavers were experienced water dwellers and he was sure they were safe. Things had changed so much since Weasel was a small kit. Nowadays the weather had got rather tricky and unpredictable. Floods and droughts were common, which made life difficult for the animals.

It was decided that returning to Hedgequarters was the best plan. And at least Weasel had his gold ring clue to go on.

Weasel, Doorkins and PPM sat atop the floating desk while the powerful otter took up towing duties. She had tied some knotted flags around the desk, pinched from the flagpoles in front of PPM's residence. Major O had cautiously promised they would be put back later on … probably!

They left PPM's house and swam along what used to be a woodland path. As they ploughed through the muddy green water, spring sunshine shone between the trees. It reminded Weasel of a photo sent by his distant cousin, Isaiah Swamp Rat. The picture had been of Isaiah's forest home in the United Swamplands

– US for short. Weasel half expected a giant alligator to thrash to the surface any moment. But maybe he'd keep that to himself – PPM and Doorkins looked edgy enough as it was.

'How deep is it, do you think, Major?' asked the Woodlands leader. She nervously prodded a paw at the murky water.

'Above my head height, without a shadow of a doubt,' the otter replied, glancing over her shoulder.

This didn't seem to improve PPM's mood at all.

The eerie silence was a little unsettling. Where had everybody got to? Weasel decided it was time to lift the spirits. 'How about a game?' he said cheerily.

Doorkins and PPM instantly seemed to drain of energy. And the Major appeared to have gone completely deaf.

If you knew Weasel, you knew he liked a game – in fact, that was an understatement. Weasel LOVED A GAME! And it was always better when his victims, er, companions couldn't escape. Such as when they were floating on a desk in the middle of a submerged wood.

'I have it. What about "SPOT THE SIGN OF LIFE"?' he suggested eagerly.

Doorkins let out a small groan. 'Did you just make that one up, Weasel?' he asked accusingly. Doorkins was not a huge game fan. A nice potter in the garden was his happy place.

'Er, why don't you go first, PPM?' the woodland super-spy proposed.

'Ah! I suppose so – what harm can it do?'

said the weary pine marten. She looked around … there was nothing … it was all as still as a very, very still thing.

Then … *SPLOSH!*

'THERE!' she called. Something had splashed into the water just a little way off. The waves rippled out in large circles.

SPLOSH … then another … *SPLOSH* … and another!

'ATTACK!' yelled Major O, pointing up into the trees.

It was hard to see anything against the low sunlight, but dark shapes appeared to flash across the sky.

SPLOOOOOSH! There was a big, heavy plop, right next to their raft-desk-type-thing.

'ROWDY REBEL ROUSERS – THEY'RE DROPPING ROCKS!' screeched Weasel.

'EVERYBODY OFF!'

Just as the animals hit the water, there was a *CRUUUNCH!* The oak desk took a direct hit, snapped right in two and sank immediately.

CHAPTER 10

'CAW-CAW-CAW ... THE ROBBER KING RULES ... THE ROBBER KING RULES!' screeched the attackers from above.

Weasel was fed up of hearing 'the Robber King this' and 'the Robber King that'. Just who in SQUAWKY-SNEEZEWEED did this character think he was? Every single dodgy thing happening in the Woodlands seemed to be in his name!

The frustrated super-spy thrashed about on a floating log. He dodged pelting stones as they splashed down all around. This lot had it in for him, no doubt.

But where had the other three got to? Like the desk, they had just disappeared! Then a large *SPLOSH* from behind him made Weasel jump out of the water like a petrified frog.

'Only us, me old mucker,' boomed the Major.

She surfaced with a droopy animal under each arm. Doorkins and Principal Pine Marten had looked better, but it was nothing a nice mug of steaming chocolatey hot chocolate wouldn't solve.

'That's a murder,' said the otter, casually dodging a rock as it plunged in the water just to her right. *KERSPLOSH!*

'WHERE-WHERE-WHERE?' exclaimed Weasel, snapping his head around.

'Not an actual murder! A flock of crows is called a murder,' she said, pointing a paw at the dive-bombing fiends.

So that's what they were. Well, Weasel had heard of a gaggle of geese and a flutter of sparrows, even a paddle of ducks – but not a murder of crows.

'CAW-CAW-CAW!' Having run out of rocks, one of the big feathered scoundrels swooped down and grabbed at Weasel. Its claw caught his jumper and lifted him from the log.

'YAAAAAAAR!' he cried in surprise.

TICKLE TICKLE

I ♥ WI6

The crow glared down at him with fierce black eyes, as it tried to flap higher.

'Weasel – crows are ticklish …!' yelled Doorkins from below.

Er, really? Yet another important crow fact he was unaware of. But he trusted his dormouse buddy without question.

'Well, here goes nothing.' He tickled away at the leg, and the crow began to cackle in the most terrible way. 'CA-CA-CA-CA-CAAAAW!'

Almost immediately the bird loosened its claws and Weasel dropped downwards.

'Ah! Didn't think of THAAAAAAAAT!' He hit the water with a big *KERSLAP!*

Shaken, he surfaced for air and another crow swooped down and scuffed the top of his head, then another.

'STEADY ON, YOU MANGY ROTTERS!' Weasel hollered.

But the birds kept swooping and the claws kept coming. His anger flared and Weasel felt the War Dance starting to brew.

But then ... BZZZZZZZ-HMMMMMM!

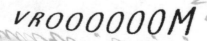

VROOOOOOM

What was that strange sound? For a moment, Weasel thought of a swarm of bees. But no … it was way too loud for a group of little nectar-munchers. Something was coming through the woods – and it was coming fast.

The dive-bombing crows scattered, alarmed by the weird noise.

A loud buzzy thing burst from the trees.

It skimmed across the water into a sharp turn and came to a halt, *SWOOOOSH*, right in front of Agent Weasel. A wave of green murky water hit him full in the face. *SLOSH—YUCK!*

When Weasel had finished spluttering, he looked up. Agent Mole and Boffin Bunny Kew sat on top of, well, a rather usual contraption.

The odd machine looked slightly familiar – half boat and … YES! Half WI6 pedal sled! Weasel had used the trusty WI6 pedal sled on a previous mission. It had been winter then and the sled had had runners for dashing through the snow. Now it sat in a low boxy rowing boat, which read 'WI6 Aqua Speeder' on the side.

'Ah-ha! You really saved us from those flying

stinkers, Mole,' cried Weasel.

The loud fans mounted on the Aqua Speeder's rear quietened as the pair stopped their pedalling.

'It's an absolute pleasure, old chap – glad we could help,' said Mole in her usual jolly tone.

Kew gave a stiff nod, not being one for small talk – or any kind of talk for that matter.

'CHITTER-CHITTER-CHAT-CHAT-CHAT' – a raspy noise came from the trees above. Weasel had heard that horrible cackle too many times today.

There, on a high branch, silhouetted against the low bright sun, sat a bird.

And even though its eyes were not visible, somehow the friends could still feel a deep piercing stare.

But by the time Weasel had rubbed the swampy water from his eyes the rascal had vanished – again!

'Who on earth was THAT?' asked Principal Pine Marten, as she and Doorkins glided up on Major O's back.

'Good question, PPM,' replied Weasel, changing to his haughty detective voice once again. 'All the evidence points to the infamous ROBBER KING.'

'Really – how fascinating. Well, I think you'd better get after him, don't you?' suggested the Woodlands leader bluntly.

'B-b-but …!' Now Weasel would almost certainly miss his pinecone crumble and ice cream. Ah well, the fate of the United Woodlands was more important, he guessed.

Principal Pine Marten climbed aboard the Aqua Speeder and Mole gave up her seat, sploshing into the water next to Weasel.

BZZZZZZZZZZ! went the propellers of the Aqua Speeder. Boffin Bunny Kew slammed the joystick to the left, released the airbrakes and with a nod and a ... *SWOOOOOOSH!*, off it went, a mighty jet of water spraying out behind. Principal Pine Marten gave a little royal wave from the back seat as the Aqua Speeder disappeared into the trees.

'Ah! Come on then, me lovelies,' sighed Major O, 'on me back.'

Weasel and Mole climbed up to join Doorkins, both soggy and cold.

'Well, I get a feeling we should go that way,'

said Weasel, pointing into the setting sun. He had no real idea which way the bird had flown, but the others seemed to think he knew what he was talking about.

With a few strokes of the otter's powerful webbed paws, they were off on the trail of the mysterious royal robber!

CHAPTER 11

The light began to fade as the small band swished along through the sunken trees. Being out at night was fairly ordinary for most woodland-dwelling creatures. But things felt spookier than usual.

Weasel shuddered as a stiff breeze blew in. He hoped to HIGH HOLLYHOCKS it wasn't going to rain again.

'Er ... did that log just move?' whispered Doorkins as they approached a rather eerie-looking dead tree sticking out of the water.

'It must be your peepers playing tricks,'

Major O whispered back.

'Hmmm, I was so sure,' whispered the dormouse fearfully.

'Why are we whispering?' enquired Mole.

'SCREEEEEEECH!' There was an ear-splitting cry.

The big otter leapt straight out of the water in shock. The others clung on for all they were worth. *SPLOSSSSSH!* she went as she flopped back down again.

'Ah! Sorry, chaps,' came a voice from the dark. 'You caught me by surprise there. Captain Barney-Barnster, Owl Force 1, don't you know?'

Owl Force 1 were the Woodlands flying squadron and all round feathery good guys. In the dusky light, it was just possible to make out a handsome beefy bird, with a wide friendly face, goggles and a brown leather flying cap.

'Well, it's jolly good to meet you, Captain,' said Weasel, shaking the owl's offered wing.

'It's an honour, Agent Weasel. I have word of some rather iffy goings on up at the Rookery,' reported the owl with a serious frown. 'Been ordered to fly you in and investigate, don't you know?'

The Rookery? Hadn't that nervy wood pigeon mentioned it before he'd flapped off? The Rookery was a mysterious place indeed. It could be found in the heart of Badger Wood, high in the branches of Big Oak – the largest tree in the whole of the United Woodlands. It was not a place many of the ground-dwelling animals ever went.

But if Owl Force 1 suspected something

dodgy, then it was good enough for Weasel. The only problem would be flying all four of them up there. In fact, it would be impossible, even for a sturdy barn owl such as Captain Barney-Barnster.

'Surely the otter and I can head to Badger Wood by water?' said Agent Mole rather surprisingly.

Major O raised her eyebrows, a little startled. 'Well, if you can save my friends from the clutches of those crows, I can put up with you on a short trip to Big Oak,' she said to Mole with a curt nod.

'Fabulous, that's that then,' said Weasel. 'My good friend and I gladly accept your kind offer of a lift, Captain.'

But poor Doorkins looked a little shaky. It was not just the thought of flying – it was that owls were usually more interested in snaffling up small rodents than giving them a lift. He stared at the large bird's talons anxiously, wondering if he might end up as his supper by the end of the flight.

'Don't you worry yourself, young mouse,' chuckled the Captain, seeing Doorkins's concerned look. 'I'm strictly a veggie owl. Never been that keen on scoffing fellow animals, don't you know?'

Doorkins heaved a great sigh of relief and the two friends hopped on the owl's broad back.

'Put these on, chaps – safety precaution, don't you know?'

The Captain passed over two khaki-coloured rucksacks. Weasel and Doorkins strapped them on – but before they could ask what they were, the owl was off with a few strokes of

his powerful
wings. Weasel
waved to Mole and
Major as they swam off
into the darkening woods.
He hoped to see them again soon – he was
getting used to having the big otter around.

They soared into the air, the ride smooth
and steady. Well, certainly much steadier than
the earlier pigeon flight. As they swooped
gracefully northwards, Doorkins seemed
almost relaxed.

Captain Barney-Barnster nodded up ahead.
Glowing lights twinkled in the trees. *That
must be the Rookery. Getting close*, thought

Weasel excitedly.

But then without warning a dark missile shot by ... *SWOOOSH* ... then another.

Something caught the end of the Captain's wing, causing him to swoop upwards suddenly.

'WE'RE UNDER ATTACK!' the owl screeched in alarm, as dark shapes darted in from all sides. Beady eyes glinted in the twilight as they flashed past.

'JUMP! SAVE YOURSELVES! Use the parachutes, don't you—' The owl was cut short as he took a sharp turn to avoid a head-on smash.

'YEEEOWW ...' cried Doorkins as he flew from the barn owl's back.

'DOOORKINS!' bawled Weasel. He dived after his friend without a thought.

What did the Captain say? fretted Weasel,

flapping his arms wildly in an attempt to hover. *The parachutes?* He looked down to see a cord dangling from his rucksack.

'PULL THE CORD, DOORKINS!' he cried down to his falling buddy. 'PULL THE CORD.'

Doorkins's parachute billowed open like a blossoming flower, while Weasel's merely ejected a mixed salad of mushrooms and dandelion leaves.

'AH, SORRY!' cried the owl as he fought off his attackers. 'MY PACKED LUNCH – DON'T YOU KNOW?'

'OH FABULOUS!' exclaimed Weasel.

CHAPTER 12

YAAAAAAAAR! Agent Weasel plummeted straight downwards, heading right for Doorkin's plump white parachute. And what could he do about it? Absolutely nothing!

FLUMMMP! Weasel landed on top of the rippling material, and it seemed it might break his fall. But then the parachute sank in the middle and completely caved in.

'YEEEEEEOWWWW! SOOOREEEEEEE, DOORKINS!' he screeched.

The pair hurtled towards the treetops. *CRACK–CRUNCH–THWUMP!* Then silence.

As Weasel dared to open an eye, he looked down – then wished he hadn't. He was clinging on to the parachute silk, which was tangled in a branch high above the ground. Generally, Weasel wasn't too scared of heights, but this made his head spin and his tummy do tipple-tails. It could only be one tree – the tallest in the whole of the United Woodlands – the mighty Big Oak, home of the Rookery.

The WI6 agent could see his little chum dangling below him. Doorkins appeared to be as still and as quiet as a, er, mouse. Weasel was about to holler at his best buddy to wake him up, but suddenly there was a loud flapping above him.

CAW – CAW – CAW – FLIPPERTY – FLAP – FLAP – FLAP ... it went.

Weasel strained to look up through the branches. It was two big black birds, crows or maybe rooks. He always found it so hard to tell them apart. They scrapped and pulled at ... EEK! Captain Barney-Barnster's smart flying-goggles! What had happened to the brave owl? Weasel dreaded to think.

'Oi, give 'em back, you scabby bog-snuffler ... CAW-CAW!' squawked one.

'CAW-CAW ... mine, mine, mine!' screeched the other.

'But, Peck – he's gonna want these for his treasure hoard!'

'I'm not letting that puffed-up popinjay have 'em, Inky.'

Hmmm, Peck and Inky, quite fitting names, thought Weasel.

'Ever since that ring went missing 'e's been giving us crows a right old load of bother.'

'It's not just you crows – us rooks have been getting it in the tail feathers as well. 'E's one angry bird.'

The pair croaked in agreement.

THE RING, thought Weasel. He rummaged inside his jumper and pulled it out. The etched letters twinkled in the moonlight. So it did belong to the rascally Robber King!

Weasel went to put it back up his jumper and suddenly fumbled, almost dropping it to the woodland floor.

PAAARP! His shock caused a loud windy-pop to sneak out. TRUMPY-TREE-TREMORS ... he was going to have to cut down on those mushrooms at breakfast time!

''Ere, what was that?' rasped the thuggish crow.

Weasel froze, expecting the worst.

'Ahhhhh! It was probably just those pesky squirrels again,' croaked the rook. 'Let's get back. He'll 'ave us plucked bare if we don't get on!'

And with that, the big gruff birds flapped off.

'PHEW!' sighed Weasel. That was too close for comfort. Looking down, he saw his little

FUMBLE FUMBLE

CORVY

I ♥ W.I.6

PARP!

buddy still dangling. Weasel carefully climbed down the parachute ropes to the silent dormouse.

'Doorkins! Doorkins!' he whispered as loudly as he dared. But the little chap seemed to be out cold.

They suddenly lurched downwards. He looked up. The parachute silk was beginning to tear!

Could he jump for it? No, too risky. Cut the ropes? No, definitely too risky. Swing? Hmmm, maybe. If they could just make it to that big branch they'd be safe … before that chute tore any more!

Weasel swung his hips in a dancey sort of way. He thought of a jaunty little tune in his head to get the rhythm. DEE-DA-DEE, DIT-DIT-DADEEDA.

It began to work. The pair swayed back and forth, getting closer to the branch with each swing, then ...
RRRRRIP!

UH-OH! Weasel's heart went to his mouth. They were going to fall!

'HEY! Grab a paw!' came an urgent squeaky voice.

Weasel looked up. A chain of three grey squirrels hung from a branch above. An adventurous-looking little female stretched out a paw. Weasel grabbed on gratefully, clutching Doorkins with his other paw, and the squirrels hauled them up.

Carefully laying Doorkins down on the thick branch, the plucky squirrel produced a small green bottle from her shoulder bag. She popped the cork and wafted it under the dormouse's nose. Doorkins shot up immediately, eyes wide as saucers.

'Wow! That was brilliant!' Weasel clapped his paws together in delight. 'What's in the bottle?' he whispered from behind a paw. Perhaps it was some kind of secret potion.

The young squirrel looked at him rather hesitantly. 'Er, essence of badger poo!'

Weasel wrinkled up his nose. 'Maybe we'll, er, keep that one to ourselves, eh!' He nudged the squirrel and glanced over at Doorkins.

'Nutter!' said the squirrel.

'I b-beg your pardon?' blustered Weasel, rather taken aback.

'My name – Nutter, Nutter Bush-tail,' she said, holding out a paw. 'This is Mother Bush-tail and Nana Bush-tail.'

'Ah! Of course,' said the WI6 spy. 'My name's Weasel, Agent Weasel.' He arched his eyebrows and flashed his best super-spy smile.

The little squirrel squealed with joy.

'She's a big fan of yours, Mr Weasel,' said Mother Bush-tail, patting the head of her kitten.

'She's going to work for WI6 when she's all growed-up,' stated Nana Bush-tail.

'Na-naaaaa …!' said Nutter shyly, embarrassed in front of her hero.

'I have absolutely no doubt she will, madam. Particularly with top-notch rescue skills like that. Hmmm, Agent Bush-tail. I do like the sound of that,' Weasel said thoughtfully, scratching his chin.

The young grey squirrel almost exploded, emitting such a high-pitched squeal of glee, it was sure to bring every dog in the surrounding neighbourhood running.

Doorkins, who was still a little groggy even after his reviving snort of badger poo, piped up, 'Blah, blah, blah … Robber King.' There was nearly a sentence there somewhere.

'Are you after that feathery villain?' asked Mother Bush-tail, all of a fluster. 'He's been trying to force us out of Big Oak for days. The shady trickster wants our beautiful home all for himself!'

'D-do you know where to find him?' asked Doorkins, coming back to his senses.

'I can show you!' blurted Nutter, bouncing up and down excitedly.

Mother Bush-tail raised her eyebrows. 'Well, she's a little 'un, but she can certainly look after herself.'

Nutter took that as a yes and immediately bounded off along a twisty branch.

'Come on, we have to go up, up, up!' she called, as Weasel and Doorkins pulled themselves together and said a quick goodbye to Mother and Nana Bush-tail, dashing after the hoppity little squirrel into almost certain danger.

CHAPTER 13

Weasel paused to listen; he could just make out a faint *DUM—DUM, DA—DA, DUM—DUM, DA—DA.* Was it the sound of his pounding heart? He couldn't tell. He'd almost run out of puff trying to keep up with Nutter Bushtail. She was completely at home dashing about in the treetops and had more zing and energy than a particularly energised zingy thing. But Agent Weasel liked this daring young squirrel. She would make a first-class WI6 agent one day.

Doorkins had also come to a halt, listening carefully with a tweak of his ear.

'That'll be the drums,' said Nutter, scampering back down the branch towards the two friends. 'He'll be having one of his, er, ceremonies again! It's not far now – come on!' And with a little flick of her tail she was speeding off again.

After more scurrying, puffing and twangy-twig-dodging, the drums became louder and louder. As Weasel looked up, there was a flickering glow through the gaps in the branches that couldn't just be the stars twinkling and the moon shining. They had to be near the top now, surely.

Then the croaky chanting began. 'GRAA-KNEE ... GRAA-KNEE ... GRAA-KNEE!'

Crouching behind a large thick branch, the three animals peeked over it. HOWLING-HIGHTREES! What on earth? A fur-raising sight lay before them.

In a massive circular dip in the tree crown, lit by flaming torches, were hundreds of crows, rooks, ravens … and many more birds Weasel couldn't identify. This must be the infamous Rookery. The birds were facing the opposite way, chanting with their wings aloft, 'GRAA-KNEE … GRAA-KNEE … GRAA-KNEE!' Two crows beat a pair of upturned buckets to a steady rhythm.

But what stood at the far end was stranger still! A tall figure almost the size of a human towered over the crowd. It looked familiar to Weasel – except for the fuzzy wig of white dandelion seeds and human-sized knitting needles it awkwardly clung on to.

'IT'S THE SCARECROW FROM THE RAPESEED FIELD! That's where it got to!'

Doorkins and Nutter Bush-tail gazed at

Weasel in horror. Had he just said that out loud? It appeared that he had – every single one of those beady black eyes had snapped in their direction.

'CHITTER-CHITTER-CHAT-CHAT-CHAT ... who's a pretty boy then?'

Oh no, not that mocking squawk again.

At the foot of the stolen scarecrow was the weirdest-looking bird Weasel had ever seen.

'A MAGPIE!' gasped Doorkins.

Of course the Robber King is a magpie! thought Weasel. Magpies had a taste for all things shiny and precious and were the biggest robbers of the lot!

The curious bird wore a purple velvet waistcoat, while a pair of piercing black eyes peered from beneath a sparkly silver robber's mask. Rather cheekily, it had the Starling Silver Nuts hung around its neck. And to top it all, it held … WHAAAAAAT! Weasel couldn't believe it. The very precious and very shiny WI6 magnifying glass! Weasel fumed. What an absolute rotter. There was no doubt this was the Robber King.

'Who dares disturb our secret gathering?' croaked the magpie.

'HAIL GRAA-KNEE!' repeated the mob of feathery minions.

'Er, just the Acorn Inspection Service,' answered Nutter as they quickly ducked behind the thick branch. 'All your nuts seem to be in order, so we'll be off now – thanks very much.'

She frantically waved Weasel and Doorkins away. But the WI6 super-spy shook with rage – he was on the verge of a Weasel War Dance. Climbing on top of the branch, he cried, 'GIVE ME BACK MY MAGNIFYING GLASS, YOU SCABBY-FEATHERED NINCOMPOOP!'

There was a loud gasp from all.

'CHITTER-CHITTER-CHAT-CHAT … who's a pretty boy then!' said the Robber King, glaring at Weasel with a cock-eyed tilt of his royal head. 'Welcome to my Rookery Kingdom. CHITTER-CHAT-CHAT … I see you remember our little ruckus.' He waved the magnifying glass teasingly at Weasel.

The furious WI6 super-spy tensed. So it had been the Robber King sneaking around

Principal Pine Marten's house. He remembered the ring, and pulled it from his jumper. 'Lost something?' he growled, holding up the sparkling trinket.

'AAAAAAAAAARGH! CHITTER-CHAT-CHAT. GET HIM, GET HIM!' screeched the magpie, flapping his wings in a complete and utter tantrum.

Weasel crouched, ready to leap at the feathered fiend. And he would have, if not for Doorkins and Nutter, who each grabbed a leg and pulled him swiftly from the branch top.

THWUMP! He clattered down bum-first, right on top of his two comrades.

The rabble of feathery fiends immediately shot forward like arrows, their sharp beaks darting at the spot where Weasel had been only a second ago. *WHOOSH—WHOOSH—*

WHOOSH! They tore overhead.

Weasel wriggled and kicked, his only thought to get the shiny magnifying glass back. Doorkins and Nutter struggled to keep hold of the squirming super-spy.

There was no choice. The dormouse cuffed his thrashing friend around the head. *BOP!* Not hard, but enough to halt his temper fit. Weasel stared at his best pal, somewhat baffled.

'Let's get out of here!' squeaked the little squirrel, pointing to the flock now wheeling round for another go.

Dragging the dazed WI6 agent by the paws, they rushed back down the twisty branches of Big Oak, the new spring growth giving little cover from the dive-bombing brutes.

As Doorkins and Nutter pulled him along,

poor Weasel got thwacked in the chops by every single twig they passed. It stung, but at least it brought him back to his senses.

Suddenly, from nowhere, a prodding beak poked between the branches and nipped poor Doorkins on the bum.

'YEEEOW!' he squealed.

'CAW-CAW-CAW!' went the flapping ruffian, alerting his fellow scoundrels to their prey. Heads and beaks barged in from all angles.

The three animals did their best to dodge and duck. But the vicious birds kept coming. These creatures were a definite pain in the backside in more ways than one.

They were coming to the end of a huge branch, and it looked like there was nowhere left to run, when ...

'There, up ahead!' It was Doorkins. He dashed along, still holding his sore bottom, pointing towards a hole in the trunk. It looked just big enough for three small animals to squeeze through.

'Well spotted, old chum,' winked the WI6 super-spy, dodging another beak.

'CHITTER-CHITTER-CHAT-CHAT-CHAT.'

It was the sound none of them wanted to hear.

Perched on a Y-shaped branch just above them was the Robber King himself. 'Who's a pretty boy then?' he squawked, with a fierce snap at Weasel's head.

Without a second thought, the super-spy dropped to his knees, sliding under the gnashing bill. *SMACK!* went the royal beak as it clacked together.

THUNK

'YEEEEOW!' hollered Weasel, forgetting how horribly knobbly oak bark was.

They plunged into the hole just in time, as a mass of black beaks lunged, missing them by a paw's breadth. *THUNK–THUNK–THUNK!* went the birds as their heads stuck fast in the small gap.

'NOOOOOOOOO!' Weasel heard the Robber King screech, as the super-spy tumbled into the darkness below.

CHAPTER 14

Suddenly Weasel's bottom thumped down on a hard surface – *OOOOOF!* He had been freefalling into the pitch dark and now began to slide, hurtling down what felt like a near-vertical tunnel. It twisted and turned through the inside of the great oak.

Then ... *WHOOSH!* Weasel flew out the end of the chute, into open space and ... *THWUMP!*

He jumped up urgently. OH GOSH! He'd done it again, flattened his good buddy Doorkins, and beneath the dormouse was poor Nutter Bush-tail.

'I am so sorry, my friends – I must watch where my bottom's going in future.' He helped them both up, dusting off their fur in the process.

But the two small creatures just stood with their mouths agape. Weasel took in their surroundings for the first time. They appeared to be in a large hollow at the centre of the tree.

But GLITTERING STICKLEBACK SCALES! This was no ordinary hollow. It was ... it was the Robber King's treasure hoard.

Mountains of precious shiny stuff piled up around them. A shaft of moonlight sneaked in from a crack high above, reflecting off the twinkling trinkets. By the height of the moon it must have been well past midnight ... *doesn't time fly when you're having fun?* thought Weasel.

'WE'RE RICH ... RICH!' cried Nutter, leaping about excitedly.

Doorkins frowned at her with a little shake of the head.

'Sorry – it's just so sparkly,' Nutter said, looking down and twiddling her paws.

'All of this treasure must go back to the decent law-abiding citizens of the United

Woodlands,' said Weasel.

'What – all of it?' asked Nutter, stroking a shiny pocket watch she'd just picked up from the pile. 'We squirrels never have much of anything – the Robber King makes sure of that.'

'All of it,' said Doorkins kindly.

Nutter Bush-tail sighed and put the watch back down.

'How on earth will we get out of here?' said Doorkins, gazing up into the high dark hollow.

Nutter, eager to please, scampered over to the wall and tapped it with a claw. It was unusually smooth and polished. She leapt up and began to climb. *WEEEEEEEEEEEE!* went the unbearable noise as she scraped back down again. Weasel and Doorkins shuddered. It looked impossible to climb, even for the skilful Nutter.

'Hmmmm,' said Weasel, thinking hard.

He didn't have to think long before Nutter cried, 'Ah-ha! I have it. What about that crack?' She pointed to where the moonlight streamed into the hollow tree.

'Not if it makes that awful noise again.' Doorkins quivered.

Nutter ignored this. 'If we stack enough treasure against the wall we can clamber up.'

'Brilliant plan!' declared Weasel. 'We might make a WI6 agent of you yet, young Bush-tail.'

The little squirrel leapt for joy, clapping her paws together.

Working as hard as a troop of woodland ants, the three animals piled up the treasure as speedily as possible. And before they knew it, they had nearly reached the opening ... but not quite.

'Hmmm, we'll have to stand on each other's shoulders,' suggested Weasel thoughtfully.

It was very rickety at the top. Doorkins stood on Weasel's shoulders and Nutter stood on Doorkins's.

As the little squirrel reached for the edge of the crack …
RUMBLE–RUMBLE … the tree began to shake!
RUMBLE–RUMBLE … Weasel's legs began to tremble.
RUMBLE–RUMBLE … the pile of treasure began to sway.

This isn't going to end well, Weasel thought.

Then … *CRAAAAAASH!* Down they went like a sack of old potatoes, leaving Nutter hanging by her paws far above.

Weasel lay on his back, head spinning. Something felt rather odd. It was as though they were moving upwards. The little squirrel, who was still dangling overhead, seemed to be quickly getting closer and closer.

He sat up abruptly.

'GET OUT OF THE WAY!' he cried, waving a paw at the young treehopper.

Just before the rising treasure hoard reached the gap, the little squirrel dived out to safety. PHEW!

But where was Doorkins?

'DOORKINS! DOORKINS!' Weasel called in rising panic … then he spotted him.

No wonder his chum hadn't answered. The diddy dormouse was only an arm's length from Weasel, but he was stuck upside down, his stubby little legs wriggling about furiously.

But the more Weasel tried to pull Doorkins out, the more his own body began to sink. The treasure was just like quicksand. First his waist disappeared, then his shoulders, and finally, only his eyes and ears were above the surface. He tried to wriggle but could barely move.

RUMBLE RUMBLE ... THUNK. The treasure hoard came to a stop.

CLUNK. A bright light switched on, blinding the super-spy for a second.

'CHITTER-CHITTER-CHAT-CHAT-CHAT. Who's a pretty boy then?' croaked a familiar voice.

Oh no! Not again, Weasel thought in despair.

CHAPTER 15

The Robber King glared down at Weasel from
a platform, backed by a number of his feathery

minions. Weasel could see the twinkling stars in the opening behind them. He realised they must be somewhere near the top of the tree again.

This must be how the villain inspects his priceless treasure hoard. No wonder the sides of the hollow are so smooth – it's probably up and down all the time!

'Where is my precious ring? CHAT-CHAT … who's a pretty boy then?' the King squawked wildly.

'Mm mm, mmm, mmm,' he mumbled in reply, his snout still covered by the treasure.

'Get them out, get them out, CHITTER-CHAT-CHAT!' ordered the magpie furiously.

CLUNK, THUNK, WHIRRRRRRRRRR!

To Weasel's surprise a large mechanical claw moved overhead, hovering above his little chum's wriggling legs. It plucked him from the pile with a *CHINK* and a *TINKLE*. The poor dormouse looked completely befuddled. He sported a good number of bracelets, necklaces and a rather fine tiara on his head. Weasel thought it quite suited his mousey pal.

The claw whirred over and dropped Doorkins at the Robber King's spindly feet …
THUMP!

Weasel frowned and twitched with anger, trying in vain to get free – how dare they treat his pal like that. Why, he would box their ears … er, did birds have ears? Weasel wasn't too sure.

WHIRRRRRRRRRR!

The claw now dangled over his own head. It was like playing grab the cuddly soft toy at the Autumn Fair. Not that he felt particularly cuddly at the moment. The claw's pincers clamped down on to Weasel's ears. YEOW! It was incredibly painful. But he was not about to show it – WI6 agents were trained not to cry in front of baddies – although his eyes did start to water a bit.

He now hung by the lugs right in front of the manic bird.

'THE RING. CHAT-CHAT-CHAT. Who's a pretty boy then?' the royal ruffian shrieked, jutting his beak into the super-spy's face.

Weasel shifted his eyes to the shiny and rather beautiful magnifying glass held in the magpie's wing.

'Ahem!' Weasel cleared his throat. 'First I'll have that, if you please?'

The magpie hopped about from foot to foot. 'AAAAAAARGH! CHITTER-CHAT-CHAT. SEARCH HIM!'

The king's lackeys began to prod the WI6 spy with their sharp beaks. It actually made him chuckle. Weasel happened to be very ticklish – particularly under the arms, it seemed.

But this tittering made the feathery felon even angrier. He screeched at his minions. 'WHERE IS IT? WHERE IS IT? Who's a pretty boy then? CHAT-CHAT-CHAT?'

'Nothing, boss – apart from this,' replied a nervous-looking rook. It was the bathroom plunger again, pulled from under Weasel's WI6 spy jumper.

'Where is my ring? YAAAAAAAR! CHAT-CHAT-CHAT.' The magpie bounced up and down like a nut on a hot plate, screeching and squawking for all he was worth.

Hmmm, thought Weasel, blocking out the noise. The ring obviously meant a lot to this villainous varmint. But where on earth was it? He'd had it earlier…

'TAKE THEM AWAY. CHAT-CHAT-CHAT,' squawked the ranting bird. 'And for your dastardly cheek you will now face the trial of A THOUSAND POOPS! CHITTER-CHAT-CHAT.'

Weasel didn't have a problem with POOP. But a thousand of them – now that was a worry.

Weasel was roughly hauled down from the mechanical claw and his paws and feet were tied. The birds forced him out of the trunk, to hop along a high twisty branch, a pointy beak annoyingly prodding in his back all the way.

He could see Doorkins, tightly wrapped in twine and tucked under the wing of a burly crow. The dormouse gave his WI6 chum a hopeless shrug. He looked more like a mouse-shaped cotton reel than the super-spy's best pal.

'CAW-CAW, come on, move it or you'll get more than a thousand poops and no mistake,' squawked the Robber King.

'Mr Fancy Pants is on his high perch today, don't you think?' whispered the crow carrying Doorkins. It nodded to the magpie proudly strutting up front with his beak in the air.

'Until he gets his precious ring back, he'll be in one of them moods,' said the other, giving Weasel yet another annoying prod.

He felt that he'd heard their voices before. Then it clicked – it was Inky and Peck, the squabbling pair they'd overheard earlier that evening. These two liked a good moan and they were not at all keen on this Robber King, it seemed.

'I don't know where you've got that ring stuffed,' grumbled the big crow into Weasel's ear, 'but you'd better un-stuff it quick – CAW-CAW – or we'll all be in for it!'

'Bring down the cage!' cried the king.

Weasel suddenly found they were back in the gathering place at the crown of the tree. As he looked up, a domed cage was being lowered from some branches far above.

The king's feathered minions perched all around, watching silently as it got closer. The cage was quite a posh one with a carved wooden base and fancy wired bars – probably a valuable antique, thought Weasel.

'HAIL … GRAA-KNEE,' cawed the Robber King, his wings held aloft.

'HAIL … GRAA-KNEE,' chanted the gathered birds in reply.

What was this 'GRAA-KNEE' nonsense all about? He, Doorkins and Nutter had heard it earlier that evening. He thought of the brave little squirrel and he hoped she was safe.

CLANK … SQUEAK.

Weasel looked up. The cage hung just above them now and he could see a sticker on the bottom. He squinted to see more clearly – it read 'Property of Granny Garrett'. Hmmm … puzzling.

Then … *CLANK* … the cage lowered to a halt right next to the Robber King. The magpie took a key from under his waistcoat, wiggled it in the lock, and the door popped open … *CLINK.*

HOVERING-HEFFALUMPS! To Weasel's surprise, it was not empty. Inside was a dazed and rather weary-looking Captain Barney-Barnster!

CHAPTER 16

Inky and Peck cackled with laughter as they launched Weasel headfirst through the door. He'd just got to his feet when ... *OOOOF!* In flew Doorkins, straight at Weasel's midriff. The pair groaned in a heap.

CLANG! The cage door shut, the key clicked in the lock, and the mini prison began to rise back up.

'Good to see friendly faces, don't you know?' croaked Captain Barney-Barnster of Owl Force 1. The poor bird lay tied and crumpled on the floor, looking as if he'd been pecked and pushed around.

'Prepare for the TRIAL OF A THOUSAND POOPS, me beauties ... who's a pretty boy then?' cried the Robber King to his feathery minions.

'Now he calls us beauties. I was a scruffy scallywag not two minutes ago!' Weasel overheard Inky whisper to Peck.

'What are they going to do with us?' Weasel asked the poor battered owl.

But before Captain Barney-Barnster could speak – 'CHITTER-CHITTER-CHAT-CHAT,' the royal magpie butted in, flapping around the rising cage. 'An excellent question, my pesky WI6 critter,' he spat viciously. 'You will be bound, gagged and placed before the statue of GRAA-KNEE.' He pointed down to Farmer Garrett's stolen scarecrow. 'Then the

fly-past of doom will begin!'

Fly-past of doom – that doesn't sound so bad, thought Weasel as the cage swung to a halt.

But the crooked bird hadn't finished. 'Each and every one of my loyal minion army will then take turns to … POOP ON YOUR HEAD!' he squawked with glee.

'Ah, I see! No, er, chance of letting us off, I suppose?' asked Weasel. It was always worth a try.

The Robber King just cackled the most awful cackle then flapped off with his feathered army in tow.

'I'll take that as a no then,' called Weasel, as the horde disappeared into the night.

'They're probably off to guzzle down more rubbish.' The vegetarian owl shuddered. 'They don't care where their food comes from. The more rubbish scoffed, the more poop pooped, don't you know?'

Weasel wrinkled his nose in disgust.

As Doorkins hopped over to check on the battered owl, Weasel felt an unexpected flutter at his ear. He stiffened in dread, guessing the magpie had returned.

But there was no 'CHITTER-CHAT-CHAT' or 'who's a pretty boy then?' Warily, he flicked his eyes to the left. And there, sitting on his shoulder, was who else but MURIEL! Muriel was Weasel's personally trained elite homing moth. Anywhere Weasel happened to be, Muriel could always find him.

She beamed her mothy little grin.

'AH-HA! My fluttery chum – I'd love to catch up but we're in a bit of a pickle. Can you help?' Weasel pleaded.

The tiny moth nodded eagerly.

'You'll find Agent Mole and Major O at the foot of Big Oak. Tell them to get up here quick-smart, we need their help!'

Muriel didn't have to be asked twice. She clicked a mothy salute and shot through the bars, spiralling down and out of sight.

As he watched the moth disappear, Weasel's eyelids began to feel very heavy. Doorkins, already slumped against the exhausted Barney-Barnster, began to snore in a cute mousey sort of way. And who could blame him? After all, it was the middle of the night and it had been a very long day indeed. Before Weasel knew it, he was off into slumberland himself, scoffing through oodles of pinecone crumble and ice cream in his dreams ... *YUMMY.*

Weasel jolted awake from his pleasant snooze. Had it been seconds, minutes, hours? It was hard to tell. One thing he did know – lying around dreaming of tasty treats wouldn't help them escape from this dangling prison. He scanned around, looking for a way out. Directly above him hung a perch with a bell and mirror attached – it might be worth a clamber up for a better view. Then his gaze was caught by a shiny water bowl on the floor of the cage – something was written on its side. The writing was very tiny – if *only* he had the WI6 magnifying glass. Weasel screwed up his eyes to read: 'This bowl belongs to Corvy'.

CORVY – the same name as on the ring. Then things began to make sense. The sticker on the cage bottom, the ring and the shiny bowl ...

'THE ROBBER KING IS GRANNY GARRETT'S PET?' Weasel blurted out loud. Granny Garrett was Farmer Garrett's mother and lived on the edge of the Woodlands.

'Ah, yes, don't you know?' said Captain Barney-Barnster, making the WI6 spy jump.

'You already knew, Captain?' gasped Weasel.

'It was those two gossiping birds – Inky and Peck. They were blabbing away on guard duty. I heard the lot, don't you know? Apparently the so-called Robber King, or Corvy as we now know him, escaped his cage one day. And Granny Garrett, being ever so upset, left it open on the garden bench in the hope he might come back. But with finding a new kingdom to rule and loads of stuff to pinch – which included the cage eventually – he did not return. But as it happened, the feathered bandit really did love his grey-haired keeper, don't you know? In her honour he stole the scarecrow from Farmer Garrett's field and created the strange statue of GRAA-KNEE –

just to remind him of his beloved owner.'

'GLITTERING GOOSEGOGS! No wonder he wants his precious ring back,' huffed Weasel. 'It must have been a gift from Granny Garrett. If only we still had it!'

'Did someone mention a ring?' asked a voice. It was Nutter Bush-tail, hanging from the rope above the cage. In her small paw glinted the Robber King's golden trinket.

'B-but how?' Weasel gaped, totally flabbergasted.

'I found it here, at the top of the tree – I didn't know it was the Robber King's,' she said shyly, offering the ring back through the cage bars.

Weasel must have dropped it in their daring getaway from the feathery horde.

Doorkins, now wide-awake from his refreshing snooze, frowned disapprovingly.

'Ah-ha! Don't fret, young Bush-tail,' cried Weasel. 'Hang on to that ring – it might just save us yet.'

The squirrel shoved it quickly back in her bag, glancing sheepishly at the scowling dormouse.

'Any chance of getting us out of here?' enquired Weasel. 'That Robber King won't be long now.'

Mind you, after their unplanned nap, he didn't have a clue how long the birds had been gone. It felt as though the sun might rise any minute.

Nutter immediately rummaged around

in her bag and pulled out ... a rather tasty-looking mushroom. 'Ah no, not that.' She rummaged again.

Weasel grinned. He liked this little squirrel. She reminded him of his young self, just slightly more squirrelly.

'OUCH!' she cried, this time pulling out a large, fierce thorn. Nutter shoved it in the keyhole of the cage door and twiddled away, trying to pick the lock.

CLICKERTY–CLACK–CLINK–CLINK

... it was proving a little trickier than expected. The birds could be back at any minute.

'What to do ... what to do?' Weasel grimaced. He leaned against the cage door in exasperation and CLANG, it suddenly flew open.

'EEK!' squeaked Nutter, just managing to hang on to the swinging door.

'Oh ah, sorry about that, young squirrel,' Weasel said. 'It must already have been, er, open. Maybe that's how the magpie escaped in the first place – a dodgy lock!'

Nutter jumped swiftly into the cage and began to undo all their fiddly knots. Who knew these bird bullies would be so good at tying stuff up?

'YEEOOOW!' cried the barn owl as Doorkins, now free, loosened his bonds.

'Sorry, Captain,' said Doorkins.

'Not your fault,' said the owl, wincing. 'My wing was injured in the scrap. I'm not up to flying, I'm afraid, chaps.'

'Hmmm,' said Weasel, puzzled. 'How are we going to get down from this pesky cage?'

'I have it!' chirped young Bush-tail. She grabbed the bits of twine that had been used to tie them up and began skilfully knotting the lengths together.

'Ah-ha! Good thinking,' said Weasel as he also began knotting twine. This little tree-scuttler would have his job before he knew it.

The rope was ready and tied to the bars in next to no time. It looked a bit short, but nothing a little hop an' wee jump at the bottom wouldn't sort out.

Captain Barney-Barnster was lowered first. They let him down carefully, so as not to hurt his dodgy wing.

Unfortunately, he did have to drop the last bit. 'YEEOWW!' he cried, crashing on to the branch below.

Next were Doorkins and Nutter. They shimmied down as quick as you like, both being top-notch tree-climbing experts. Weasel swiftly followed. He had just begun his descent when … 'CAW-CAW-CAW!'

YICKERTY-YIKES, the birds were back! On the horizon where the dawn light now glowed, a black cloud of feathery fiends raced towards them.

They hurtled in from all angles. Some swooshed right past the WI6 super-spy, some sliced at the escape rope with their razor-sharp beaks. He had no choice: it was back up to the cage quick-smart.

Weasel quickly scrambled in through the cage door, as – *PING!* – their getaway rope snapped and fell to the branches below. He tumbled to the floor, exhausted. Suddenly, things began to wobble and shake frantically. Weasel looked up. Oh no, it was Inky and Peck. Peck was living up to his name by pecking wildly at the rope holding the cage. And it had begun to fray dangerously!

'CHITTER-CHITTER-CHAT-CHAT-CHAT. Who's a pretty boy then!' Uh-oh! If there was one voice he didn't want to hear at that particular moment.

'Guess who's back? CHAT-CHAT-CHAT?' it croaked menacingly.

CHAPTER 17

The Robber King gripped the cage bars, glaring down at the WI6 agent. His black beady eyes glanced towards the open door.

'Oh no you don't, young fella-me-lad!' Weasel leapt up, wrenching the door shut. *CLANG!*

And just in time too – Inky, Peck and the magpie lunged through the bars. They snapped and poked at the poor super-spy's paws. YEEEEOW! Weasel bravely held on with all his strength. He was surprised at Inky and Peck. Their dislike of the royal rotter had been clear, but it didn't stop them having a good old chomp now!

Suddenly the pesky birds began to tug viciously at the bars of the door. One thug would have been enough, but three of the scruffy scoundrels was too much for Weasel to hold and he had to let go.

TWANG! As the door sprang open, all three birds shot off the cage and plunged downwards, squawking with rage.

'WEEEEASEL!' came a cry from somewhere close by. He snapped his head round. It was Nutter Bush-tail, clinging to one of the branches that the bird cage dangled from. 'THE RING!' she called, holding up the Robber King's golden trinket. She had to duck and dive as some of Corvy's minions swooped in, viciously grabbing at her with their claws.

AAAAAARGH, if only Weasel had it. It might give him some power over this rascally thief. Fortunately, the puffed-up magpie hadn't spotted the little squirrel. The birds who'd been flung off the cage door came back at Weasel with a vengeance. And not just three – there were loads now, all pecking and snapping. He got a right royal nip on the bottom through the cage bars. OUCH.

This pushed the WI6 agent a paw too far. His bum began to shake as he spun and kicked out, jumping through the door. The rotten rook who'd bitten his backside took a thwack under the beak. 'OOOOF-CAW-CAW.'

The Weasel War Dance was in full flow!

The WI6 super-spy dodged and kicked as more feathery minions plunged in. He scurried so rapidly over the outside of the cage, their

jabbing beaks couldn't catch him.

Feathers and fluff flew everywhere as Weasel biffed and bashed the hysterical mob. But there were just too many of them. Holding on to a bar, he slid back down the side of the domed cage, latching on to the wooden rim at the bottom.

The big mass of squabbling birds pecked and flapped at each other, trying to work out where Weasel had got to … while the cage swung wildly to and fro – the fraying rope ready to snap!

But the Robber King had had his beady eye on Weasel the whole time. 'CHITTER-CHAT-CHAT. Who's a pretty boy then?' The royal rascal soared upward, ready to dive at the woodland spy.

'WEEEEEASEL!' called Nutter again. She hurled the gold ring towards the cage. For a moment it looked as though the ring might fly straight past Weasel. But the War Dance

meant his reactions were quicker than normal and he shot out a paw, plucking it from the air.

'SQUAAAAAWK!' The villainous bird was almost upon him and his beady eye clocked the ring. 'CHAT-CHAT-CHAT!' he screeched.

Weasel tossed the gold band, rather casually, into the cage.

SWOOOOOSH! The magpie darted in and fell upon his lost treasure.

CLAAANG! Weasel slammed the door shut. And with his super War Dance strength, he bent a bar across to hold it closed. This dodgy door would not open again!

Without warning, there was another jolt and the cage dropped a few centimetres. The scrapping birds above squawked and flapped away, just as – *PING!* – the rope snapped and the cage fell.

Weasel, not fully aware he was toppling down head over heels, shook his noggin to clear the War Dance haze. Then *THWUMP!*

It appeared he'd made another soft and pillowy landing. This was getting to be a habit. And a pretty good one at that! He was lying on what felt like a feathered quilt.

There came a low groan. 'UUUUUUH, don't you know?'

'Ha! Captain Barney-Barnster!'

Without a thought for his injured wing, the big brave barn owl had shot like a lightning bolt to save his super-spy friend. He now lay crumpled on a knobbly branch, wincing with pain.

'Thank you, my fearless chum. How's the wing?' asked Agent Weasel, helping the poor bird to his feet.

'Ah! It's nothing, just a painful rump to go with it now, don't you know?' The plucky Owl Force Captain straightened his bent tail feathers.

'SQUAAAAAWK! CHIT-CHAT-CHAT!' the Robber King shrieked angrily from within the cage, which now teetered dangerously between two spindly branches. 'ATTACK, me beauties. Commence the FLY-PAST OF DOOM!'

The screech and flap of a hundred birds was deafening. 'CAW-CAW-CAW!' The horde swooped straight for Weasel and his owl friend.

'RUUUUUN!' cried Weasel, but poor Barney-Barnster was plumb tired out. They struggled along the twisty branches as the birds quickly gained on them.

Then *SPLAT–SPLAT–SPLAT*, the POOP began to rain down!

CHAPTER 18

Weasel and Barney-Barnster ducked under the closest branch as the POOP splattered everywhere. What had these birds been eating? Whatever it was, it smelt toxic – very toxic indeed! Weasel just hoped Doorkins and Bush-tail had found shelter from the stinky downpour.

He racked his spy brain for a way out. Surely at some point the birds would just run out of poop?

And then, as if by magic, the splattering stopped!

'Looks like they're all pooped out, don't you know?' The big owl grinned.

Weasel and Barnster cautiously poked their heads out from beneath the leaves. They were in the gathering place at the tree's crown again.

'CAW-CAW-CAW!' The flock was flying around in a mad panic. They crashed and bashed into each other in an attempt to get away.

What was going on?

'GRAA-KNEE – GRAA-KNEE!' the Robber King cried. Still trapped in the posh antique bird cage, he held his wings aloft to the big scarecrow statue.

Weasel quickly looked up. 'HOPPING

HOLLYBUSHES! That scarecrow is turning its head! And raising an arm!' The sight sent a shiver down the super-spy's back.

'Do not fear, my minions. CHAT-CHAT-CHAT!' squawked the Robber King. But the minions did fear, and they all began to fly off.

That was when Weasel noticed the Starling Silver Nuts, hanging on a branch next to where the cage had landed.

'YIKES, won't be a minute, old chap,' Weasel cried to Barney-Barnster and dashed off, the necklace the only thing on his mind.

The droppings lay thick and all around, and he tried to dodge them as best he could. His heart fluttered. It was a long way down if he fell out of the Rookery hollow. Weasel skidded to a halt in the slimy mess and snatched the nuts.

'SQUAAAWK, CHITTER-CHAT-CHAT!' screeched the Robber King in rage. He had just got one precious thing back and now lost another. 'You will pay for this, pesky WI6 agent. CHAT-CHAT-CHAT who's a pretty boy then?'

'Surely it's you who should pay for this,' snapped Weasel. 'Pinching stuff from innocent animals – you should be ashamed.'

A loud *CRACK* caused them to look up.

Uh-oh! The scarecrow had started to tip, its arms flapping as if to keep upright.

'YEEEEEOW!' shrieked Weasel, diving clear just in time.

CREEEEEEAK—BOOF went the scarecrow's head, directly on to the cage. The force pushed it straight through a gap in the branches and down to the floodwater below.

'NOOOOOOOOOOO! CHITTER-CHAT-CHAT!' cried the magpie as he plunged towards the water. The cage landed with an almighty *SPLOSH*. Floating on its wooden base, it bobbed around a bit, then drifted off towards Garrett's Farm.

'I will have my revenge, Agent Weasel. Who's a pretty boy then … CHAT-CHAT-CHAT!' the despicable magpie screeched, his voice getting fainter as he was propelled away from the tree.

'Say hello to Granny Garrett for me, won't you, CORVY!' Weasel waved as the cage disappeared into the morning mist. Then he got a sudden whiff of the toxic bird poop. 'SUFFERING STINKHORN!' He winced, looking down at his splattered pullover. 'That's another jumper well and truly finished then.'

Weasel felt a little flutter on his shoulder. It was Muriel.

'Whatever happened to you, my fluttery friend?' Weasel asked, beaming away at her. 'I thought you were off to get help?'

She nodded her little head over to the toppled scarecrow.

'Ah, glad to see you in one piece, me old mucker!' said a voice. It was Major O. She climbed out of the scarecrow's jacket, covered in straw, followed by Mole, Doorkins and Nutter.

'Well, I never. That was some puppet show you put on,' chortled Weasel. 'And you got rid of that rotten Robber King. Thank you, my friends.'

He looked down and saw the poopy Starling Silver Nuts still gripped in his paw. But, oh no, the magnifying glass! He couldn't return to Hedgequarters without it – it was the most precious thing in the WI6 detective kit. And he really, really liked it. He looked around wildly.

'CAW-CAW. Looking for this?' It was Inky

and Peck. Inky held the sparkly detective tool in her beak as they flapped in.

The team tensed, ready to take on the two birds and any others that happened to come their way.

'You were trying to bite my noggin off only moments ago,' growled Weasel.

'It's a peace offering. CAW-CAW. We're glad to be rid of that wicked magpie really,' said Peck, looking shame-faced. 'We promise to return all the treasure to the woodland animals, no matter how long it takes. CAW-CAW.'

'Hmmm, well, see that you do,' said Weasel, taking the magnifying glass from Inky. He signalled to his comrades to stand down.

'And don't you forget that scarecrow – it goes back where you found it,' squeaked

Doorkins crossly, wagging his paw at the two sheepish birds.

The crow and rook bowed awkwardly, then flew off to join their ragged flock in the treetops some way off.

'Come on, me 'andsome, we've got the WI6 Aqua Speeder waiting down below,' said Major O. 'No doubt there'll be some hot chocolate and biscuits back at HQ.'

Weasel's eyes lit up. *Ah ... it'll be grand to get home, he thought with a smile.*

CHAPTER 19

By the time the team returned, everybody was up and about. Their journey back to HQ had been a rather slow one. The floodwaters had dropped and they'd dragged the Aqua Speeder across the woodland floor for the last part of the journey. Not the victorious entrance they'd hoped for, but at least they were back.

HQ teemed with bustling woodland creatures. Most of the poor things had been flooded out of their burrows and dens, but with the sun shining bright and the blossom blooming, all seemed in quite good spirits.

Nutter Bush-tail was in complete awe of the magnificent hedge – she had never been to this side of the Woodlands before. Her little squirrelly face gaped in amazement. Weasel could see she was now more determined than ever to become a WI6 spy some day.

'HO! WEASEL, young fella me lad,' called a friendly voice from the top of the hedge. It was Father Beaver.

Mother Beaver popped her head out between the twigs. 'Get yourself up 'ere for a big hug and mug of hot chocolate, me dear boy,' she bellowed.

Weasel waved happily, relieved to see his good friends safe after their ordeal.

'AHEM?' came an enquiring cough from the platform just above the Beavers' heads. It was H, Principal Pine Marten and Boffin Bunny Kew. The Boffin Bunny eyed the magnifying glass Weasel held in his paw. *He's probably wondering where the rest of his WI6 detective kit is*, thought Weasel … *At least I rescued the best bit.*

PPM looked back to her smart and confident self after a bit of a wash and change of clothes. Something Weasel could do with himself, particularly after all that stinky bird poop.

'Well done, er, team,' H said hesitantly. She was never that comfortable dishing out the praise. 'We have reports that the Robber

King is now locked up and back with a rather overjoyed Granny Garrett. We won't be seeing him again for a while.'

'HURRAH!' cheered the animals, more in relief than happiness. It was never a good thing to see a wild animal behind bars, but maybe this time it was for the best.

'Thank you, my fine creatures,' chipped in Principal Pine Marten. 'Your first-rate efforts have saved the day! And we have a well-deserved surprise for you on top deck.'

Well, this is certainly a turn-up for the books, thought Weasel. *We're usually sent packing or get another mission slapped in our paws.*

H frowned; she wasn't one for giving out awards.

Weasel, Captain Barney-Barnster, Major O, Doorkins, Mole, Nutter and Muriel made their way up through the hedge, chatting excitedly all the way. As they stepped out on to the platform, they were astonished by what they saw.

A steady stream of crows, rooks and ravens were flying in to the top deck, dropping clawfuls of bright shiny objects on to a large pile.

'THE ROBBER KING'S TREASURE HOARD!' cried Weasel happily. Good old Inky and Peck had kept their promise.

'Come on, my dears, tuck in,' said Mother and Father Beaver. They stood beside a table covered with mugs of steaming hot chocolate, tea and, to Weasel's utter delight, a magnificent display of cake and biscuits. And guess what? They had his favourites – stripy icing and all.

Doorkins gave Weasel a nudge. 'Wasn't

there something else?' he whispered behind his paw.

'W-what? Oh yes, I almost forgot!' He rummaged up his WI6 spy jumper and pulled out the STARLING SILVER NUTS.

He turned to face PPM, as did all the animals. He held up the nuts and placed them over Principal Pine Marten's bowed head. She sniffed and wrinkled up her snout. Hmmm, poopy or not, she was glad to have them back.

'I, er, thank you, Agent Weasel,' she said.

'CAW-CAW-CAW!' Suddenly there was an awful flapping commotion behind them. The animals whipped round and – oh what a shock! The table of glorious sweet things was empty. There was barely a crumb left!

'CAW-CAW-CAW!' came a racket from the nearby field. There stood the scarecrow, back in its place. And sitting all along its sticky-out arms were the crows, rooks and ravens. They were chomping and cackling happily, finishing off the last of the animals' party tea.

'AAAAARGH, you pesky rascals!' cried Weasel.

Inky and Peck sat on the scarecrow's head – grinning the widest grins you have ever seen.

'Ah well! Canteen, anyone?' suggested Weasel happily. 'I heard there's some pretty scrummy pinecone crumble and ice cream on the menu.'

And with that, the friends strolled off paw in wing to stuff their hungry faces!